Her time was up

Poised with one foot on the edge of the bed, she stroked the moisturizing cream her leg absently as her mind rep... the day and the man she'd... suffused her... sweetness of...

The barely per... connecting door opening fr... its upward stroke. A shiver ... onition feathered her shoulders an instant before she heard Peter's sharply indrawn breath.

For a long moment her mind went absolutely blank, then she reached for her nightgown. Shielding her nakedness with the next-to-useless sheer material, she stood glaring at him from eyes chilled with challenge.

"What do you want?" Patricia immediately regretted the demand. The answer was obvious.

"I want my rights as your husband."

Available from Joan Hohl

LADY ICE

Business consultant Peter Vanzant had earned his killer reputation by taking risks, and his latest deal would have him laughing all the way to the bank... and to his bedroom. An arranged marriage to Langdon and Company's ice-princess vice president— a merger of brilliant minds and perfect bodies.

ONE TOUGH HOMBRE

Something had happened to ex-cop Josh Barnet on the streets of the city, something bad enough to turn a dedicated crime fighter into a ranch hand. At first Nicole Vanzant heeded that haunted, don't-get-too-close look she saw in his eyes, but the time had come for answers....

FALCON'S FLIGHT

Flint Falcon had started with nothing to his name but bad memories and big dreams—and now he had it all: power, money and the hottest hotel-casino in Atlantic City. But there was one thing he wanted that he'd never let himself have—the woman who reminded him of his worst days....

Joan Hohl

LADY
ICE

Silhouette Books

Published by Silhouette Books
America's Publisher of Contemporary Romance

SILHOUETTE BOOKS

ISBN 0-373-48325-2

LADY ICE

Copyright © 1987 by Joan Hohl

Available from Joan Hohl

LADY ICE
ONE TOUGH HOMBRE
FALCON'S FLIGHT

One

"The world is run by men and it's held together with rhetoric."

Donna Bathshore gazed at her boss in confused shock. "What do you mean, Ms. Lycaster?" Donna asked hesitantly, not at all sure she wanted to hear the answer. At twenty, Donna liked men, really liked them.

"Exactly what I said." Patricia Lycaster pushed her chair away from her desk. Rising with unstudied grace, she moved to the wide window that overlooked the spacious parking lot. "Because women have left the running of the world to men for centuries, the masculine gender has just about managed to screw up just about everything.''

Donna's pretty face registered surprise at Patricia's harsh tone and rough language. As a rule, Patricia's voice was low, well-modulated and cultured. But then, Donna was fairly new to the position of private secretary to the vice president in charge of office services in the firm of Langdon and Company, Consultant Engineers. Donna had a lot to learn about her job *and* her boss.

Her big blue eyes wide and filled with both admiration and a tinge of envy, Donna stared at Patricia's long slender back, her gaze drifting down the length of her shapely legs to narrow ankles and feet. A sigh of longing whispered silently through Donna's bow-shaped lips as her glance traveled back to Patricia's smoothly coiffured, natural blond hair. Small and gently rounded, Donna felt more than willing to forfeit ten years of her young life in exchange for the tall svelte, ultra-cool appearance of the woman staring pensively out the window. In profile, Patricia's features could only be described as delicately classic. Her brow was high and smooth, her cheekbones prominent, her nose narrow and perfectly straight and her jawline, while slightly squared, was finely delineated.

As Patricia turned from the window to smile cynically at Donna, the younger woman automatically smiled back and stared in mute awe. Viewed full face, Patricia Lycaster's beauty was breathtaking. Tinted a pure red, Patricia's full lips seemed to invite the exploration of a male mouth, her high, tip-tilted breasts appeared to entice a broad male palm and her trim body had the look of waiting for a special mate.

All of which was disconcerting to Donna, who had already learned, through discourse with her boss and the company grapevine, that Patricia Lycaster actively disdained the male of the species.

"Take this company, for instance."

Donna blinked and turned her attention to the cool, low-pitched voice of her boss. "This company?" Donna chewed on her full lower lip. Office gossip had provided her with information about the company's financial difficulties. Liking her job and Patricia Lycaster, Donna had hoped the rumors were exactly that—office rumors. She was now afraid she was about to learn the truth; she was right.

"Yes, this company." Patricia walked back to her desk with her customary litheness. "You've heard that the company has some problems?" Arching one pale eyebrow, Patricia eased her slim body into her desk chair. When Donna nodded, she continued softly, "And what have you heard?"

Donna's teeth punished her lip a moment, then she blurted, "I was told that the company is in financial trouble."

"Amazing." Patricia's lips curved wryly. "For once the grapevine is basically correct."

Donna suffered an uncomfortable sinking sensation. Darn it! She not only needed this job, she wanted it. At the same time, she couldn't help but wonder why Patricia Lycaster was discussing the subject with her secretary. Even though Donna felt rather privileged, she also felt confused. Patricia cleared up both questions with her next statement.

"Of course, the situation is not beyond saving... with the proper guidance." Patricia's startling gray eyes narrowed. "I intend to fight for the proper guidance at the board meeting this afternoon." A brief but sincere smile moved her lips. "Please bring me the file on Bettina Manweller, then you may go to lunch."

Donna scurried into her own connecting office, a grin of admiration lending an impish look to her gamine face. Donna had prepared the file on Bettina Manweller. She knew the woman had an excellent reputation as a business consultant and had virtually saved many firms from bankruptcy. By taking her secretary into her confidence, Patricia Lycaster had taken a giant step in squashing the rumor making the rounds on the company grapevine. Donna could hardly wait to get to the employees' lunchroom after delivering the requested file to her boss.

A satisfied smile tilted the corners of Patricia's lips as she watched Donna's hasty retreat from her office. Her highly buffed, unpolished nails tapping the file folder, Patricia imagined she could hear the self-importance in Donna's voice as she condescended to apprise her fellow workers that the rescue of the company was imminent.

Though Patricia had wanted to squelch the rumors, she firmly believed in Bettina Manweller's ability to steer the company out of the red and into the black financially. Now all Patricia had to do was convince the board of directors.

Patricia was marshaling her arguments when a soft tap sounded on the door. Moments later her mother, Margaret Langdon Lycaster, stepped into the office.

"I looked for you in the dining room," Margaret said, closing the door quietly behind her. After Patricia's father's death six months ago, Margaret had taken over the position of president of the company. "I should have realized you'd forgo lunch to prepare for the board meeting."

"Mother, you know I never eat in the executive dining room." Her soft lips twisted. "The extravagance and waste are appalling."

Sighing deeply, Margaret sank onto the chair Donna had recently vacated. "I know." Her shoulders moved in a helpless shrug. "Why your father ever insisted upon a French chef and a haute-cuisine menu for lunch every day, I'll never understand. But, once begun, a system is hard to break."

"What you mean is," Patricia said grittily, "your executives would scream bloody murder if they were suddenly denied pan-fried squab for lunch."

"Yes, well . . ."

"Yes, well, nothing," Patricia inserted when Margaret's voice trailed away. "This company's lifeblood is gushing out through the coffers while

its executives dine royally and hand in mind-
boggling expense forms." Standing abruptly, she
strode to the window and back, impatience taut-
ening her slender body. "Mother," she said
roughly, "something must be done. The firm
your father founded, and was so proud of, is going down the drain."

"I know!" Margaret snapped sharply, then
repeated in a gentler tone, "I know. That's why
I came in to see you. I, ah, have a suggestion."

Patricia was immediately wary. The only time
her mother hesitated over making a suggestion
was when she knew Patricia would not be in
favor of it. Pondering on what sort of mach-
inations were simmering behind the bland expression on her mother's still-beautiful face,
Patricia composed her features.

"And that is?" she asked in a chillingly remote tone.

"I want your permission to arrange a marriage between you and Peter Vanzant."

"You want to do what?" Patricia stared at her
mother in stunned amusement. Of all people,
Margaret knew her daughter's feelings about
marriage. Surely Margaret was leading up to
some sort of a joke.

"I said," Margaret repeated distinctly, "I want to arrange a marriage between you and Peter Vanzant."

Patricia didn't blink. She didn't frown. She regarded her mother coolly. "And who is Peter Vanzant?" A wry smile shadowed her lips. "If I might ask, that is?"

"Does it matter?" Margaret retorted calmly.

Patricia's composed facade slipped—just a little. One perfectly shaped eyebrow peaked. "What are you getting at, Mother?" A tiny, warning smile played over her lips. "And it had better be good."

Margaret wasn't in the least intimidated by her daughter's attitude. Relaxing against the back of the chair, she drew a cigarette from the gold case she always carried with her and lit it before responding.

"I'm getting at saving this company."

"At my expense?" Patricia asked sweetly.

"If necessary," Margaret returned bluntly.

Patricia studied her mother silently for several seconds. She was not insulted or hurt by Margaret's answer. Patricia knew her mother would do anything short of breaking the law to save the firm her father had worked so hard to build. And Margaret knew that Patricia was just as determined to save the company as she was. But marriage? Patricia repressed a shudder.

"I'm convinced there must be an explanation—a very good explanation—for your idea hidden somewhere inside your pretty head," Patricia said slowly. "Would you care to elaborate?"

Margaret smiled. "Actually, there are several reasons for my suggestion." Margaret drew deeply on the cigarette before continuing. "First, it's time you were married."

Patricia's laughter was a soft interruption. "Time? Since when is there a time to be married?"

Margaret was not amused. "You are twenty-eight, Patricia!"

Patricia nodded solemnly. "Irrefutable fact," she agreed, containing a smile.

"And a wedding ring on your finger would keep the overeager men at a distance," Margaret added.

"Knowing the morals of most men, I doubt it," Patricia murmured.

Margaret was beginning to look a little frayed around the edges. "Peter Vanzant could save this company." A victorious smile on her peach-tinted lips, she crushed out the half smoked cigarette. Margaret was making a Herculean effort to cut down.

"Indeed?" Patricia looked unimpressed. "At the risk of repeating myself, who *is* this Vanzant person?"

Margaret stiffened, knowing that her daughter was going to prove difficult. The very fact that Patricia had referred to the man by his last name told Margaret her daughter was going to dig her heels in. When Patricia dug in, the grooves went deep, usually into some male's self-esteem.

"Peter Vanzant is probably *the* most respected and sought-after business consultant in the world." Forgetting her vow of one cigarette per hour, Margaret lit another smoke before continuing. "And, if you didn't have this blind spot in all things concerning men, you'd know about him." She exhaled a cloud of blue-gray smoke. "Everybody in the business world has heard of Peter Vanzant!"

"Ta, ta." Behind the drawled flippancy, Patricia's mind was ticking like a finely crafted timepiece. In truth, she had come across Peter Vanzant's name while garnering information on Bettina Manweller, but she certainly was not about to admit it to her mother. Leaning back in her chair, Patricia gave the deceptive impression of boredom. "If this *man* is so very well known and respected," she chided softly, "I can't imagine why you'd think he'd be interested in a marriage arrangement." Her gray eyes lightened. "Or is the poor man old and ugly?"

Margaret's sudden laughter danced on the room's controlled air. "Old and ugly? My dear, misguided, man-hating girl, Peter Vanzant is thirty-six years old and handsome as the very devil!"

"You know him?" Patricia queried disinterestedly.

Margaret shook her head. "I haven't met him, no. But I've seen pictures of him and I've spoken to him on the phone." Her eyes rolled dramatically. "That man has the sexiest voice!"

"Ho, hum." Lifting a long-fingered, slender hand, Patricia fabricated a yawn. She really wasn't interested in sexy male voices. She definitely was interested in knowing why her mother had had occasion to speak to the man with the sexy voice at all. A trickle of unease slid the length of her elegant spine. "Mother," Patricia said too softly, "please don't tell me you have already broached this ridiculous subject of a marriage arrangement with this man."

Margaret bolted upright in the leather-covered chair, her sky-blue eyes wide with shock. "Patricia Marie Lycaster! Do you think I'm an utter fool?" Since she didn't expect an answer, she didn't wait for it. "I wouldn't have dreamed of discussing this with Mr. Vanzant before speaking to you."

"Good thing, too. My answer is no." Considering the subject closed, Patricia glanced at the slim gold watch encircling her delicately formed wrist. "We have twenty-five minutes until the meeting." Raising her head, she smiled at her mother. "Would you like a cup of tea or coffee?"

"No." Margaret started to shake her head, then paused. "Well, all right, I'll have coffee." Again she paused, eyeing her daughter warily. "Patricia, I really do think you should give my suggestion a little more thought."

Patricia didn't hesitate in the process of rising to get the coffee. She glanced at her mother as she walked to the tiny kitchenette connected to her office. "What's to think about?" she inquired blandly. "I don't want to get married, ever." Filling two pedestal cups with the aromatic brew, she turned to deliver one of them to her mother. "Not to this Vanzant person or any other man."

"And the company?" Margaret asked sharply. "You'll never convince me you don't care if the company goes under."

"I wouldn't begin to try." Patricia laughed, momentarily filling the room with a delightful sound. "Like you, I'd do anything possible to save this firm."

"But that's what I've been trying to tell you!" Margaret exclaimed in exasperation. "Peter Vanzant *can* save this firm."

Patricia tapped the oval nail of her forefinger on the file lying on her desk. "So can this woman," she said gently. "Bettina Manweller. Have you heard of her?"

"Yes, of course," Margaret murmured dismissively. "I understand she's very good."

"Precisely." Satisfaction could be heard in Patricia's attractively husky voice. "And I intend to convince the board members of the necessity of hiring her to direct us out of this financial quagmire we're in."

"It won't work." As if she were suddenly uncomfortable, Margaret shifted in the chair and toyed with the curved handle of the cup.

Alerted, her internal alarm ringing, Patricia carefully placed her cup on the gleaming surface of her desk. A sneaky suspicion crawling through her, she stared into her mother's eyes. "Why won't it work?"

"I, um, I've already hired Peter Vanzant," Margaret admitted in a rush.

Patricia frowned. "But the board..."

"I spoke to each member privately," Margaret whispered.

"Mother!" Margaret cringed at Patricia's harsh tone. "How could you do that? You're saying the board meeting will be nothing more than a formality!"

"In a word, yes." Very slowly, Margaret lifted her head. "The privilege of rank, you know." At that moment the similarity between mother and daughter was apparent. Fearlessly, Margaret faced the obvious anger roaring through her daughter. And, in a fury, Patricia was a sight to behold.

Gray eyes stormy as clouds accompanying a tornado, Patricia shoved back her chair and sprang to her feet. Her body taut with rage, she stalked around the room, her movements unnatural, jerky. "Damn!" Biting out the curse, she whirled to face Margaret. "That was below the belt." Her stance defiant, she glared into her mother's calm eyes. "Were you aware I was having a file worked up on Bettina Manweller?"

"No, I was not." The response was immediate and adamant.

Patricia didn't question her mother's veracity, simply because she knew Margaret would no more lie to her than she would ever consider lying to her mother. A defeated sigh whispered through her lips.

Patricia didn't like having to fall in with her mother's plans—she didn't like any of it. But she would go along with it; she had no choice. However, she had no intention of backing down gracefully.

"This whole deal reeks of coercion, Mother," she said accusingly.

Margaret smiled faintly. "I feel positive that while your father was in command, the board members were conversant with coercion."

"Oh, undoubtedly." Patricia's tone was laced with sarcasm. "But I'm not referring to the board members." A mocking smile curved her lips when Margaret contrived an innocent expression. "I'm referring to your original suggestion."

"About arranging a union between you and Peter Vanzant?"

Mocking smile in place, Patricia slid her hands into the slash pockets of her suit skirt, looking for all the world like the female prototype of the cool businessman. "The very same." Her tone matched her smile.

"I wouldn't dream of trying to coerce you into marriage!" Margaret protested in a scolding tone. "I merely thought it would be the perfect solution to several problems."

A frown drawing her blond eyebrows together, Patricia gazed at her mother curiously. "I'm beginning to get the feeling that I've missed some vital bit of information here. If the deed is done, and you've already secured the services of Vanzant, why even suggest a legal arrangement?"

"Well, Mr. Vanzant's services are dreadfully expensive," Margaret replied inanely.

"Mother." Patricia's tone was so pleasant it was scary.

"Oh, all right!" Her actions unconsciously mirroring her daughter's, Margaret flung her slender body out of the chair and proceeded to pace the deeply piled, gold-toned carpet. Unlike her daughter, she came to an abrupt halt before an ornamental oval mirror on the wall opposite the desk. Lifting her chin, she angled her head to the right, then the left, searching for flaws in the flawless face reflected there.

"Not bad for a woman of fifty," she murmured. "If I do say so myself."

"Mother, how long has it been since you heard me scream?" Patricia's mildly voiced question caught Margaret unawares.

"Why, not for years and years." Shifting her gaze, Margaret met Patricia's eyes in the mirror. "Why?"

"Would you care to hear me scream now?" The gray eyes piercing Margaret's remained rock steady.

Margaret got the message. Swinging around, she gave a helpless shrug. "I know." She sighed. "I'm a vain woman."

"With a tendency to procrastinate," Patricia drawled. "The subject is Vanzant—" she arched one brow "—remember?"

"Why do you persist in calling him by his last name?" Margaret closed the distance between herself and her daughter.

Patricia looked slightly surprised: her mother seldom became ruffled, it was bad for the com-

plexion. "But that's his name, isn't it?" she
asked reasonably.

Margaret took the final step that brought her
to within inches of Patricia. Of equal height, and
almost identical appearance, they might have
been taken for sisters. At the moment, there was
very little identical about them. Margaret looked
thoroughly irate, while Patricia's calm composure revealed nothing of her thoughts.

"I'm convinced that merely hiring *Mr.* Vanzant is not enough. He'll work much harder at
saving this company if he has a vested interest in
it."

Though she was positive of the answer, Patricia had to ask the question that burned on her
tongue and made her blood run cold. "You're
proposing to offer him a piece of the company?" For the life of her, Patricia couldn't raise
her voice above a whisper.

"Naturally!" Margaret snapped, immediately drawing a deep breath to calm herself; her
daughter was trying at times. "That is how a
marriage of convenience is arranged. Each party
receives compensation for the contract."

"Well, naturally!" Patricia's patience finally
snapped. "But I can't help but wonder exactly
what compensation I would receive from such a

contract—except a husband I don't want, of course." Her eyes glittered like new steel.

Margaret's gently curved breasts heaved with her sigh of exasperation. "You really do have a blind spot about men, Patricia. If you didn't you wouldn't be so dense at this moment." She betrayed her annoyance by raking long fingernails through her exquisitely styled blond hair. "You would receive an equal share in the company you claim answers every one of your life's needs!"

Patricia went absolutely still as her mother's words settled in her mind. Then, confusion lending a smoky haze to her eyes, she blurted out, "You're prepared to turn over control?"

Margaret nodded regally. "I'm prepared to bow out of the corporate picture completely." Her blue eyes sparked a warning. "If and when I'm convinced the company is in capable hands."

Now Patricia *did* feel a sense of hurt. "And you're convinced that my hands are not capable?" It required every ounce of willpower she possessed to maintain a steady tone.

"Your hands alone?" Margaret smiled softly. "Darling, if I left you on your own, they'd tear you apart."

"They? You mean the competition?"

"Yes," Margaret agreed, her tone hardening, "and they—the majority of our own people. If you can step around your ego, you'll realize I'm simply giving you facts."

Though Patricia drew herself up straight, she accepted the truth of her mother's statement. Working together, she and her mother were barely managing to keep the firm floundering. Alone, either one of them would fail. *But a husband?* Patricia shivered at the repulsive thought.

"Well, do I have your permission to approach Mr. Vanzant?"

Feeling suddenly trapped, a sensation not unlike that of crawling things invading her stomach, Patricia tried to delay answering and grasped at the straw labeled *board meeting*. Glancing pointedly at her watch, she straightened first the skirt then the jacket of her tailored suit and adjusted the jabot attached to her teal-blue blouse.

"It's time for the meeting," she said briskly, striding to the door. "We'll have to continue this discussion later."

Laughing softly, Margaret followed her out of the office, teasing gently, "My daughter, fearless in any business situation and an absolute coward in any personal encounter with men."

Pretending she didn't hear her mother's chiding remarks, Patricia hurried through the outer office and along the wide corridor to the plushly carpeted boardroom.

The meeting was, as Patricia had predicted it would be, a formality. Although the board members dutifully went through the motions, in the end they outvoted Patricia's proposal to engage the services of Bettina Manweller and approved Margaret's counterproposal to hire the renowned Peter Vanzant. The salary he'd demanded made Patricia blanch, but bothered the board members not at all.

The sham of the meeting over, Patricia lingered at the long conference table until the room was empty of all but Patricia and Margaret. Her voice cracking with righteous indignation, Patricia repeated the exorbitant figure the board had meekly agreed to lavish on Peter Vanzant.

"I thought the idea was to hire someone to *save* the firm money," she said sarcastically, "not speed up the drain-off process."

"That is the man's usual compensation," Margaret argued reasonably.

"Mother, the figure is ludicrous!" Patricia protested. "No single consultant is worth it—even if he does his consulting while standing on his head autographing potato chips! The man is obviously a rip-off artist!"

"Patricia!" Margaret did something she rarely ever did: she raised her voice in anger. "Mr. Vanzant is an expert in his field. And I believe he can salvage this company if—I said *if*, mind you—he has a strong enough reason to do so." With a visible effort, she forced her tone to a more even level. "You would do well to consider my suggestion if *you* really want to save this company. I will need an answer today."

"Today?" Patricia blinked in astonishment. "But why today?"

"I have an appointment to meet with him later this afternoon—" she smiled dryly "—ostensibly to engage him as a business consultant. I want your permission to make him another offer as well."

"But wouldn't his acceptance constitute a conflict of interest?"

"Exactly." Margaret smiled sweetly. "He can only accept one of the offers. I'm gambling our Mr. Vanzant will go for the whole ball of wax."

Cornered, Patricia stared at her mother. Long seconds ticked away as she weighed and measured her options. There weren't many. In fact, there weren't any. The deciding factor was her intense desire to make Langdon and Company viable again.

"A marriage of convenience?" Her mouth was so dry, Patricia hardly recognized her own voice.

"A marriage of convenience," Margaret agreed quickly, sensing victory. "You get half my controlling stock. He gets half the stock. And I get a long-overdue vacation." Barely breathing, she waited for Patricia's answer.

Patricia couldn't force the words out of her mouth. Nodding sharply in agreement, she spun on her heel and stalked from the room, making a beeline for the sanctuary of her own office. In her haste, she missed the tender smile that curved her mother's beautiful lips.

Back from lunch, Donna was sitting at her desk in the outer office, a dreamy expression on her face, her eyes bright as she stared into space. She didn't even notice Patricia when she strode into the room.

"Donna?" Patricia came to an abrupt halt when the young woman failed to respond.

"Donna!" she said in a sharper tone.

"Oh, Ms. Lycaster!" Donna smiled sheepishly. "I didn't see you come in."

"Obviously," Patricia drawled. "Aren't you feeling well?"

The girl sighed sheepishly. "I'm feeling fine," she sighed again. "I think I'm in love."

Patricia raised her eyes as if asking for help. "You fell in love over lunch?" she questioned dryly, disbelievingly. "Donna, that's simply not possible." Dismissing the very idea, she headed for her office.

"But you haven't seen him, Ms. Lycaster!" Donna protested, grabbing her pad and trailing after Patricia as she walked into her office. "He's absolutely . . . absolutely!"

"Well, that explains everything," Patricia drawled mockingly. "Now can we get to work?"

"He's tall and slim, but with a muscular build, if you know what I mean." Dreamy smile back in place, Donna dropped into a chair. "He's dark all over—hair, eyes, skin." She sighed once more. "And he has this . . . this dark, brooding look." She shivered. "Delicious."

Patricia scoured her memory for a young male

employee who might fit Donna's description and came up blank.

"Who is he, Donna?" she asked with forced patience. "What department does he work in?"

"I don't know. I never saw him before." Donna smiled at her mistily. "I think he must be a god."

Two

A god? Oh, God! Patricia was torn between laughter and a groan. Turning away to conceal the smile that persisted in a twitch at her lips, Patricia strolled to take up her familiar thinking stance at the window.

"I think he's a visitor."

Patricia went absolutely still. Could it be? she thought, hoping it wasn't, knowing it was.

"A visitor?" She turned to level a cool-eyed glance at Donna.

"Hm." The younger woman had a faraway look. "He was escorted through the employees'

lunchroom by your mother's assistant, Mr.
Cummiss.''

"I see.'' Patricia's gaze drifted back to the sun-
sparkled pane of glass. She didn't notice the dust
motes prancing within the bright afternoon rays.
What she saw, and understood, was that Peter
Vanzant had been in the building all the while
Margaret was backing Patricia into a corner.

How long would it be before her mother made
the proposal to the man? Patricia mused, nar-
rowing her eyes. Knowing her mother's swift-
strike philosophy, she decided it would not be
long at all. Her lips tightened rebelliously.

A marriage of convenience. A shudder rippled delicately down her spine. How utterly ar-
chaic! A god. Patricia grimaced. A dark,
brooding god. The shudder intensified. He might
be handsome and godlike but Patricia definitely
did not want to marry him or anyone else—not
now, not ever.

Her only hope lay with the faint possibility
that the man would scorn her mother's proposition. A dry smile flickered on her lips, writing
finis to that particular hope. Patricia knew, instinctively, that Peter Vanzant would jump at the
offer. He was a man, wasn't he?

* * *

The man stood easily at the wide expanse of window behind the large, glass-topped desk in Margaret's spacious office. His tall, elegantly slender body was advertised advantageously by a three-piece, hand-tailored suit in a pewter-gray shade, set off by a pale blue shirt and red and gray striped tie. Framed by the window, the picture Peter Vanzant made was enough to cause a flutter in any woman's heartbeat, including that of Margaret Langdon Lycaster, who was fifteen years his senior.

Less than thirty minutes had elapsed since Peter had returned to Margaret's office from his guided tour of the company. Most of those minutes had been used by the amenities, the offering and accepting of coffee, etcetera. Now, by his very direct stare, Peter was making it plain that he was ready to talk business.

"Won't you have a seat, Mr. Vanzant?" Margaret produced her most devastating smile as she indicated the velour-covered sofa in the far corner of the large room.

"Thank you." Peter acknowledged the smile with a barely discernible curve of his thin, very masculine lips and sauntered across the room. After politely waiting for Margaret to seat herself, he lowered his long body onto the cushion one removed from her. Angling his body toward her, Peter arched one midnight-dark eyebrow questioningly.

"As I'm sure you realize," Margaret began slowly, "I invited you here for the purpose of acquiring your expertise as a business consultant."

Peter allowed a brief nod of his head to suffice as an answer.

Margaret moistened her suddenly dry lips, intimidated by the imposing appearance of the man. "But," she finally continued, speaking a little faster now, "I changed my mind in the interim." Expecting a reaction from him, she paused. Other than a mildly inquiring gaze, Peter displayed no reaction.

"However," she went on more rapidly, "I do have a proposition to offer you." Strangely breathless, Margaret fell silent, waiting.

"A proposition?" His voice complemented his appearance. It was low, smooth and, knowingly or unknowingly, sexy as hell. "What sort of proposition?"

"A proposal of marriage." Margaret firmly believed that there was only one way to get to the point, and that was to get to the point. Having blurted out her thoughts, she regarded him from behind a facade of composure, and curled her fingers into the palm of her hand.

Peter didn't laugh aloud or scoff or sneer. With just a hint of a smile, he returned her gaze steadily. "You wish to marry me?" Like his smile, there was a hint of teasing in his tone.

"I!" Margaret blinked, then laughed. "No, of course not!" Belying her fifty-one years, her smooth, creamy cheeks bloomed with a becoming pink tinge.

"I'm too old for you?" Peter's dark eyes gleamed with devilry.

"Too old?" Margaret frowned, then, realizing that he was attempting to ease the tension, smiled naturally. "Thank you, Mr. Vanzant," she murmured, suddenly deciding she liked this man...liked him and wanted him for Patricia—for more than the purpose of saving the company.

This time Peter returned the smile in earnest, revealing glistening white teeth that contrasted sharply with his dark skin. Margaret's heart beat a fast tattoo. Obviously satisfied with the results of his compliment, he stretched his long legs out in front of him, crossing them at the ankles in a pose of ease and relaxation.

"Now," he said encouragingly, "would you care to explain that rather intriguing proposal?"

Respecting his intelligence, Margaret briefly, succinctly outlined her proposition to him. Peter remained silent, an expression of interest on his handsome face throughout her recitation. She was nervous and speaking very fast by the time she summed it all up.

"So, there you have it. I'm proposing a marriage between you and my daughter." Her smile lacked sparkle. "A marriage of convenience, if you will."

"Whose, I wonder?" Peter's dark gaze pierced Margaret's last shred of composure.

"Wh—uh, what do you mean?" she asked hesitantly.

Peter smiled chidingly. "You are proposing to sign over your controlling shares of stock, in equal amounts, to your daughter and me on the day we sign a legal marital merger." He tilted his head. "Is that correct?"

"Yes."

"What's in it for you?" Peter asked bluntly.

Margaret's reply was equally blunt. "Freedom."

"From the position of president? From the firm? From your daughter?" Peter shot the questions at her rapidly.

Margaret's response was as swift. "Yes. Yes. Yes."

Some time later, Peter strolled through the wide corridor on the floor that housed the executive suites. His lips were quirked with amusement. Contrary to what he had expected that morning, the day was proving both interesting and entertaining.

How often in one lifetime could a man expect to be offered a routine job, only to find himself the recipient of a proposal to marry a woman he'd never even set eyes upon?

The smile on Peter's lips grew into a near grin as he contemplated the question. To Peter's way of thinking, Margaret's proposition was not only outdated, it was outlandish. Yet it did have its intrigue value.

Peter's eyes narrowed as he approached the suite bearing the name of his quarry on the solid oak door. Patricia Lycaster, Vice President.

Staring narrowly at the name emblazoned on the door, Peter thought about the woman who bore the name. What was she like, he mused, this woman who had agreed to become his wife sight unseen? Was she rich, well-bred and as ugly as sin? Peter dismissed the consideration with a shake of his head, unwilling to believe that a woman as refined and beautiful as Margaret Lycaster could produce an unattractive child. Even if the daughter didn't quite measure up to the mother in looks, she would be a long way from ugly.

On the other hand, if the woman was rich, well-bred and passably attractive, why agree to an arranged marriage to a man she didn't know from Adam?

Damned intriguing. The grin faded from Peter's lips. Deciding the time had come for investigation, he reached for the shiny brass doorknob.

The young woman playing guard dog in the outer office was pretty with a rounded figure, and at the moment appeared stupefied as she gaped at Peter slack-jawed and wide-eyed.

"Ma—may I help you, sir?" Donna's tone hinted at a willingness to do just about anything he might suggest.

Peter concealed a grin with some effort; in truth, he wasn't unused to his masculine effect on the opposite sex. Peter accepted his attractiveness with gratitude and used it ruthlessly.

"Yes." He gave her his most charming smile. "I'd like to see Ms. Lycaster, please."

Donna's soulful look assured him that, as far as she was concerned, he could see anyone his heart desired to see. Anyone, that was, except Patricia Lycaster. Donna might be fairly new at her job, but she'd been at it long enough to learn that it was dangerous to disregard orders. Ms. Lycaster had left word that she was not to be disturbed.

"I, uh, she's pretty busy now, sir, I . . ." Donna's breathless voice trailed away as she seemed to get lost inside the alluring darkness of his eyes.

"I think she'll see me." Peter smiled gently. "Buzz her and tell her Peter Vanzant requests an audience with the royal princess," he said in a conspiratorial tone.

"I can't say that!" Donna raised a hand to her mouth to smother a giggle.

"No?" Heavy disappointment colored his tone. "Then I suppose you'd just better tell her I'd appreciate a few minutes of her time." Peter's smile was designed to annihilate all female objections. It worked—as it always had in the past.

Donna depressed a button on the interoffice machine and relayed his request while gazing at him with her limpid eyes. Peter's smile disappeared as the fluttery young secretary ushered him into the vice president's presence.

She was standing at the window behind her desk, her back to him—her very straight, stiff back.

"Mr. Vanzant, Ms. Lycaster," Donna said, nervously and unnecessarily.

"Thank you. You may go, Donna," Patricia said, without bothering with the courtesy of turning around. "And I still do not want to be disturbed." She emphasized the word *still* lightly but tellingly.

Warned by her cold stance, Peter felt anger stir inside and felt his features lock into an unrevealing mask. So this was the woman who'd agreed to a marriage of convenience with him. Peter's eyes narrowed. What kind of game was she playing, making him wait until she deigned to face him? Peter's lips tightened. Turn around, honey, he thought dismissively, let me have a look at you.

As if she had the ability to read his mind, Patricia slowly eased around to face him, her chin high, her gray eyes sharp as steel with challenge. Although it didn't show, Peter had the uncanny,

uncomfortable sensation of having received a
hard blow to his suddenly taut stomach.

Ugly? Passably attractive? Peter smothered a
derisive burst of laughter. Patricia was, in a
word, stunning. And that was precisely how Peter felt, momentarily stunned. He hid it well. His
step brisk, he crossed the carpeted floor, extend-
ing his hand when he got to within a few feet of
her.

"Peter Vanzant, Ms. Lycaster. I believe your
mother mentioned me to you?" Annoyed at his
initial reaction to her looks, Peter attempted to
add a cynical edge to his low, even tone.

Patricia's composed features set, as if suddenly coated with ice. Her eyes took on a flint-
like color. "Yes, I believe she did, Mr. Vanzant,"
she concurred with a like cynicism, placing her
palm against his.

A shocking sensation not unlike an electrical
charge crackled throughout Peter's system, tingling every nerve ending in his body and sound-
ing an alarm in his mind. Releasing her hand
abruptly, he stepped back, covering his retreat by
indicating a chair with a negligent gesture.

"May I sit down?" Overcompensating for his
unusual response, Peter's voice was coldly remote. Inside, he was a seething mass of conflict-

ing emotions. Damn it! he raged, it hadn't been that long since he'd been with a woman. Why was his libido doing cartwheels?

"Yes, of course." Patricia's cool tone interrupted his thoughts. "Would you like a cup of coffee?"

"I'd prefer a stiff drink," Peter said honestly. "Scotch if you have it."

"Certainly." Patricia moved to the wet bar along the far wall, her easy stride revealing none of the sensations vying for supremacy inside. She felt offended by his abrupt, dismissive tone. She felt insulted by his cynicism. She felt shaken by her own body's reaction to the light touch of his hand. Her skin still burned from the brief friction of his palm sliding on hers. And, most amazing of all, there was a tremor in the fingers that gripped the outrageously expensive bottle of whiskey. Startled, Patricia stared in wonder at her hand; her fingers never trembled!

"Not joining me?" Peter asked mockingly, as she handed the cut-glass tumbler to him.

"I detest the taste of whiskey," Patricia said bluntly, returning to the bar to pour a cup of coffee for herself.

Peter's lips curved wryly. "To each his own form of poison." He tilted the glass in a parody of a salute, then drained half the contents in two deep swallows.

The whiskey hit Peter's throat, then his stomach, like a wave of fire. Instead of dousing the flame touching her had ignited in him, the alcohol added fuel to the blaze. Mentally detaching himself from the sudden throbbing demand of his body, Peter sipped at what was left of his drink and gazed at the woman across the desk from him.

The desk was wide enough to accommodate two comfortably.

Peter nearly choked on his whiskey at the errant thought. Then again, he mused, skimming a glance over the gleaming desk surface, the idea did have merit. The image evoked increased Peter's thirst considerably. For a fleeting, arousing instant, he had an erotic vision of Patricia, beneath him, her pale skin translucent against the dark wood, her gray eyes stormy with passion instead of annoyance.

The image was gone in a flash, but the unsettling effects lingered to puzzle Peter. He had desired many women, yet never, on first meeting a woman, had he experienced sensations even remotely similar to this.

His detachment shattered, Peter drained the last of the Scotch in his glass and set it aside. He gazed at the woman on the other side of the desk.

"Your mother made me a startling offer this afternoon," he said starkly. "I believe you're aware of the particulars?" Peter studied her composed features for a hint of what she was thinking. There was none. Patricia was a cool one, he had to give her that.

"Yes, I'm fully aware of all the particulars," Patricia responded frostily, and observed him from eyes that resembled chips of gray ice. She didn't like this Peter Vanzant, but then, she didn't really *like* any man. There were a certain few she gave a grudging respect to, but she didn't like any one of them. Most particularly, she didn't like the way he'd been visually undressing her since he'd entered her office. It was demeaning and disgusting and... Patricia searched her mind for a descriptive word. When *exciting* came to mind, she literally froze.

Exciting? Fear stiffened Patricia's spine as it crept from the base of her nape. There wasn't a man alive capable of stirring her to excitement!

"And Margaret was telling the truth when she assured me of your agreement to her proposal?"

"I want this company very badly, Mr. Vanzant." Using the flat statement for an answer, Patricia folded her hands on the desk in front of her and studied him unemotionally.

Oh, yes, this is definitely a cool one, Peter decided, returning her stare directly. *One might even go so far as to accuse Patricia of being downright cold. Was there any warmth in her at all?* he wondered, feeling strangely challenged.

"Then the offer *is* convenient," he responded dryly. "For I've suddenly discovered that I want it very badly, too."

Big surprise. Patricia almost smiled, but prudently kept the jeering thought to herself.

"Then you have accepted the proposition?" she asked, her tone even.

"No." Peter gave a brief shake of his head. "I requested permission of your mother to look at the company accounts before making a decision." He thought it wise not to tell Patricia that he had also wanted to check her out as well. The company's financial situation had come as no surprise to Peter; Patricia had. He was confident of his ability to whip the company into shape . . . but it was the idea of whipping Patricia into shape that suddenly appealed to Peter.

Holding her icy stare, Peter reached unerr-
ingly for the phone on her desk. As his fingers
grasped the ivory receiver, he raised one dark
eyebrow questioningly. "With your permission?"

Within minutes the deed was done. The deal
was struck. A date had been set.

Her icy composure concealing a growing sense
of panic, Patricia heard herself agreeing to become Peter Vanzant's wife in two weeks and
three days.

Two weeks and three days! The panic inside
Patricia spread at an alarming rate. Was she
completely out of her mind? she wondered, a little wildly. She didn't want to get married. And,
having been in his presence only half an hour, she
most particularly didn't want to marry Peter
Vanzant.

Patricia's frozen exterior revealed none of her
internal turmoil. Appearing calm to the point of
being disinterested, she listened to Peter's wedding suggestions. Then, coolly, precisely, she told
him her own preferences. A brief battle ensued.

"I want no fuss, no bother," Patricia insisted
when Peter argued for a church wedding, followed by a large reception. "I do not want any
frills."

"My dear Patricia," Peter retorted rather sca-thingly. "We are discussing our marriage, *not* the weekly expedition to the supermarket." Surging to his feet, he measured the width of her office with long, impatient strides.

"I am well aware of what we are discussing," Patricia enunciated coldly. "And, though it may be spring, we are certainly not talking about love in bloom here." Patricia ached to take up her stance by the window, but there was no way she'd share the floor space with him. "The subject is convenience," she gibed, "not compulsion." Her taunt earned her a glare from behind narrowed eyes.

"Oh, there's compulsion," Peter said too softly. "At this moment, I feel compelled to grab you and shake some sense into you."

"I strongly advise against any such action." Patricia's voice was coated with ice; her gray eyes contained shimmering crystals of frost.

Goaded by her defiant look, Peter took one purposeful step toward her. Whether or not he would have actually carried out his threat, Peter would never know, as Margaret saved the day, and the situation, by entering Patricia's office unannounced at that moment.

Always sensitive to the vibrations around her, Margaret paused midway between the door and Patricia's desk, her blue eyes shifting from Peter to Patricia.

"Don't tell me, let me guess." Margaret sighed. "You've run into a snag already?" Her gaze still moving between the antagonists, Margaret continued into the room. As she gracefully sank onto the chair nearest Patricia's desk, she sighed again. "I'm waiting," she prodded, spearing one, then the other, with a deceptively calm glance.

"Ladies first," Peter drawled sardonically, inclining his head in a mockery of respect to Patricia.

Angrier than she could ever recall being, Patricia went absolutely rigid, every outraged sense demanding retaliation. Still, her voice remained steady, her tone subzero.

"As I suspected," she said directly to her mother, "this *idea* of yours is not going to work." With insulting deliberation, she turned her back on Peter. "Hire the man as a consultant if you must, but forget about handing over your stock and deserting this sinking ship."

"Patricia!"

Margaret's gasp covered an instant of indecisiveness in Peter that was caused by the conflicting desires to laugh and curse at one and the same time. He wanted to laugh when he realized how well Patricia had read her mother's true motives. The urge to curse was a result of being presented with Patricia's back.

"Did you ever spank her when she was young?" The hesitant instant over, Peter tossed the rhetorical question at Margaret as he sauntered to the bar to refill his glass with the excellent Scotch.

Margaret's lips twitched out of control as she saw her daughter's spine grow impossibly straight. "Darling, please do try to relax. I fear your back's about to snap," she murmured soothingly, slanting a sparkling glance at Peter.

Returning her amused gaze, Peter raised his glass and one brow at Margaret. "Can I get you something to drink?" he asked politely, easing into the role of host as effortlessly as a handsome mallard would ease into an inviting pool of water.

"Why, yes, thank you." Margaret grinned at him and gained a friend and ally for life. "I'll have what you're drinking . . . but with a lot less Scotch and a large splash of club soda."

Standing by the window, Patricia was literally shaking with suppressed fury. She opened her mouth to snap out a request that both her mother and Peter leave her office just as Peter added more fuel to the fire.

"Perhaps I can make up for your previous laxity," Peter mused aloud, strolling to Margaret to hand her her drink, "after Patricia and I are married."

Peter's comment brought Patricia around to face him. Not even attempting to conceal his amusement, Peter smiled at her with devastating effect. At least Margaret was devastated; she gazed up at him in the same awed manner as Donna had earlier. However, Peter's charm was lost on Patricia, who was obviously not impressed.

"One can hardly make up for the sins of the parents with a wife one doesn't have," she observed with the bite of dry ice. "Can one?"

"Then you're definitely going to renege?" Peter asked quietly, leading Patricia to wonder if he hadn't very cleverly manipulated both her and her mother. But, before Patricia could respond in the affirmative, Margaret sprang from her chair, her face pale, her lips trembling.

"Patricia, you agreed!" Margaret stated in a genteel tone.

Beginning to feel cornered again, Patricia sighed in exasperation. "Mother, would you condemn me to a life of dissension and argument?" Revealing emotion for the first time, Patricia raked her fingernails through her short, elegantly swept-back blond hair. "We can't even agree on the type of wedding we'll have. How do you expect us to manage a marriage?"

"Oh, Lord, is that what this contretemps is all about?" The strain drained from Margaret's face. "What *is* the problem with the wedding arrangements?"

"He wants to make a splash."

"She wants to sneak away like a thief in the night."

Peter and Patricia spoke simultaneously, and likewise both fell silent. Her expression reflecting that of every harried mother since the beginning of time, Margaret spared the couple an impatient glance.

"You want to elope?" Margaret demanded of Patricia in a tone of sheer disbelief.

"Of course not!" Patricia's cool was melting rapidly. "I simply suggest we have no fuss."

"But you want a big, splashy affair?" Margaret shifted her attention to Peter, who was very calmly sipping his Scotch.

"Not at all," he corrected. "I'm in favor of a small quiet wedding." Finishing his drink, Peter set the glass on Patricia's desk with a determined-sounding thunk. "But I insist on a large reception." His voice hardened with arrogance. "My family will be served."

"Not at all," he snorted. "I'm in favor of a simple, quiet wedding." Throughout dinner, Peter set the pace on . . . on aspects with a deft . . . concentrating mostly . . . that I had on a large table. His voice lingered with a sudden . . . Patty family will be served. . . .

Three

———

My family will be served.

Peter's statement echoed sardonically, if silently, inside Patricia's head. Her body slick with sweat from vigorous exertion, Patricia tightened her lips into a grim line and threw herself into the dancercise routine.

"Now turn and stretch and kick and kick and kick!"

The instructor's voice droned on, unnoticed by Patricia who was working harder than she ever had since joining the class, at her mother's urging, three months ago.

Arrogant son of a . . . banker. Patricia kicked out angrily. She had to be out of her mind to even consider joining forces with Peter Vanzant. He had obviously been spoiled by the handsomeness of his looks and the fawning attention of far too many women, all of whom were not overly bright, in Patricia's unspoken opinion.

Less than a week to go. The realization of time running out shivered through Patricia's heated body. A sensation too similar to panic to be acceptable clawed at her throat. Following the program automatically, Patricia's thoughts backtracked over the previous week and a half.

Incredible as it now seemed, she had passively allowed Peter and her mother to make all the arrangements for the swiftly approaching nuptials.

The word "nuptials" sent another shiver skittering along Patricia's spine.

I don't want to get married! Patricia was forced to clamp her lips together to keep from crying the protest out loud. The claws of panic gripped her throat. When she realized her breathing pattern was rapidly approaching the stage of hyperventilation, Patricia walked off the exercise floor. Her mother found her in the shower room minutes later.

"Is something wrong, Patricia?" Margaret frowned, patting at her glistening face with a shocking-pink hand towel.

Is *something* wrong? Patricia gulped down a burst of wild laughter. *Everything* is wrong! Shaking her head, she continued to peel off the black bodysuit clinging to her skin.

"No," she denied, in a commendably steady tone, she decided, considering her frame of mind.

"But then why are you changing?" Margaret asked, peering at her suspiciously. "The class is only half over."

Patricia sighed. "I'm changing because I'm tired, Mother."

"Tired?" Margaret's eyes narrowed as she examined Patricia's pale cheeks. "You never get tired." Stepping to her, Margaret pressed her palm to Patricia's forehead. "You're not coming down with something, are you?"

Yes, I'm afraid I'm coming down with a severe case of Vanzantitis.

Touched by her mother's genuine concern, Patricia kept the observation to herself. Instead, she smiled gently and shook her head again. "No, Mother, I'm sure I'm not coming down with something." Stepping out of the bodysuit, she wrapped a large towel around her. "It's been a rather hectic week." Patricia's smile was wry. "As you know," she continued, reaching out to grasp Margaret's hand reassuringly. "I simply want to go home, have a quiet dinner and fall into bed." She turned away, heading for the shower stalls. "Don't concern yourself about me," she tossed over her shoulder, her gray eyes gleaming with seldom-revealed devilry. "You go back to the class and work that cellulite off your thighs."

"Patricia Lycaster!" Margaret called after her indignantly. "I haven't an ounce of cellulite, and you know it!"

Patricia's only response was a ripple of teasing laughter.

"You're getting married next week!" Nicole Vanzant's normally soft voice held an edge of shrill amazement. "When did all this happen?" she demanded. "Good grief, I've only been away for two weeks!"

"If you could manage to keep quiet for a few minutes, I'll be happy to fill you in on what you've missed while you were gone." Peter smiled at his younger sister with wry indulgence.

"Actually, darling, you haven't missed much of anything," Carolyn Vanzant drawled, somewhat insultingly.

His dark eyes glittering coldly, Peter sliced a glance to where his mother sat at the end of the long dining-room table. His lips tightened at the sight of her beautiful face, set into lines of amused disdain. As his gaze clashed with Carolyn's, she raised her wineglass in a mocking salute.

"Carolyn, please, our daughter is waiting for an explanation," Paul Vanzant murmured chidingly from his position at the far end of the table. "Peter, enlighten your sister." The request was the closest Paul ever came to an order when speaking to his son. Paul knew better than to attempt issuing orders to Peter.

Insolently shifting his gaze from his mother to his sister, Peter allowed a smile to gently curve his lips at the expectant look on Nicole's exquisite face.

"It's very simple, love," Peter said softly. "I've met the woman I wish to spend the rest of my life with." His deep voice didn't falter over the lie. "Her name is Patricia Lycaster. We are going to be married next week."

Peter's smile evaporated as he watched the shock ripple across Nicole's face. His chest rose slightly in a silent sigh. Peter hated upsetting Nicole, but it couldn't be helped. As in every facet of his life, when a decision was reached, Peter carried it through with ruthless determination. Now he had made the decision to marry and, come hell or high water, Peter would be a married man one week hence.

Nicole's expression altered, changing from shock to stunned blankness. "But, Peter, how did this all happen?"

"Too quickly to be believed," Carolyn said before Peter could respond.

Though a muscle flickered in Peter's taut jaw, he ignored his mother's caustic comment—as he'd been ignoring just about everything concerning his mother for over ten years, ever since learning of her infidelities and her proclivity for young men. Because of his mother, Peter rarely visited his father's house. This evening he'd made an exception. He had accepted his father's invitation to dinner to apprise both Paul and Nicole of his plans.

"Yes, it happened quickly." Peter infused warmth into his tone. "I met Patricia and immediately fell in love." The muscle in his jaw jumped again at the unladylike snort that came from the other end of the table.

"Love," Carolyn said in a scathing tone. "How sweet."

"Mother," Nicole whispered pleadingly.

"Carolyn!" Paul said sharply.

Peter didn't bother to spare her as much as a glance.

"Well, isn't it sweet?" Carolyn asked mockingly. "I mean, really, here we all were, convinced that Peter was absolutely incapable of loving anyone but himself."

Angered by the stricken look on his sister's face, Peter slowly turned his head. The coldly dismissive glance he swept over Carolyn brought a flare of deep color to her expertly made-up cheeks.

"Are you challenging me, Carolyn?" Peter inquired in a deadly mild tone. The use of her first name was an ongoing insult; he had discarded the respectful term *mother* when he'd lost all respect for her.

"Peter." With that one warning word, Paul sounded exactly like his son, cold, determined, ruthless.

With a show of supreme unconcern, Peter transferred his attention to his father. "Sir?"

"Oh, God." Nicole's low moan robbed Paul of the opportunity to chastise his son. "Why must every family meeting deteriorate into an argument?" she wailed.

"Why? Because I insist on attending these meetings," Carolyn inserted. "Isn't that right...*son*?" she taunted.

"Precisely...Carolyn," Peter jabbed back coolly.

"Enough!" Paul's tone had a cutting edge. "Peter, you were explaining the situation to Nicole. Continue," he ordered in his best bank-president voice. He turned his drilling stare on his wife. "Please refrain from comment until Peter is finished," he said in a soft tone that belied his hard stare. Carolyn merely nodded and flicked one hand negligently.

Smothering another sigh, Peter found a tender smile for Nicole. "You'll like Patricia, I think." *I hope*, he amended to himself. "She's not only beautiful, but very independent and, from all I've heard, an extremely capable business-woman."

"Which probably explains the attraction," Carolyn murmured.

"I have arranged for you to meet her tomorrow evening," he went on, ignoring his mother. "If that's convenient for you?"

"Yes, of course." Nicole frowned. "But where?" Her eyes grew wary. "Here?"

"No." Peter smiled. "We've all been invited to join Patricia and her mother, Margaret, for dinner at Margaret's home."

Nicole slid a glance at her mother. Peter's smile turned dry as he read Nicole's expression. "Yes, Carolyn has condescended to join us."

"Actually, I can't wait," Carolyn drawled in a tone of utter boredom. "I'm literally gasping to meet the woman foolish enough to marry the man with the reputation of being ruthless in his dealings with women."

"*Actually*—" Peter deliberately emphasized his use of his mother's favorite word "—I am very generous with women." The smile he gave her was chilling. The scraping sound of a chair being pushed away from the table drew his attention back to Nicole.

"Where are you going, dear?" Carolyn asked the question on Peter's lips.

Nicole shook her head distractedly. "I don't know, but I can't take any more of you two slicing at each other."

In a rare moment of unison, alarm flared in the three pairs of eyes staring at Nicole. The three spoke in unison.

"I'm sorry, darling. Please sit down. I promise I'll control my tongue," Carolyn urged contritely.

"My dear, stay. I'll restrain your mother and brother," Paul coaxed gently.

"Sit down, love, I'll behave myself," Peter assured softly.

As Nicole turned slightly to slip back onto her chair, a faint hairline scar was brought into sharp relief by the shimmering chandelier above the table. Peter winced at the mark on her otherwise flawless right cheek. The faded line was evidence of the car accident Nicole had been involved in several years previously. The incident had claimed the lives of the other two people who were in the car and had put an end to her successful modeling career.

A surge of compassion for his sister washed away the antipathy for his mother. Peter smiled easily at Nicole as she settled into the plushly padded chair. "Do you have any other questions?" he asked.

Nicole met his gaze directly. "Yes, one. Do you really love her?"

"Yes." Peter didn't hesitate an instant over the blatant lie. He knew that admitting the truth of the situation between Patricia and himself would hurt Nicole, and as far as Peter could prevent it, nothing would ever hurt Nicole again. "We have many interests in common," he continued, thinking that the important one was the company founded by Patricia's grandfather. Denying himself a cynical smile, he added, "Anything else?"

A teasing smile played over Nicole's lips as she nodded. "When would you like me to vacate the town house?"

Peter stared at Nicole blankly as her query sank in. He had thought of everything—except Nicole's residency in his house. Peter had offered his house to Nicole some months ago, when she had decided to rejoin the human race and had declined their parents' pleas to move back home.

After her terrible accident four years before, Nicole had withdrawn into herself mentally, and to Peter's vacation house in Maine physically. On her return to Philadelphia, Peter was still very concerned about her. Needing to keep an overseeing, if distant, eye on his sister, Peter had talked her into moving into the town house he used infrequently, due to the fact that he worked out of offices he maintained in New York City, and lived in the high-rise apartment he owned there.

Now, having made the decision to take up permanent residence in Philadelphia and concentrate his expertise on the firm he'd control jointly with Patricia, Peter had already set plans in motion to close his consultancy offices and sell his apartment. And, somehow, while taking care of business *and* making all the necessary arrangements for the wedding, Peter had completely forgotten the effect it would all have on Nicole.

The silence lengthened in the elegant dining room while Peter ruminated. He was about to respond to Nicole when Carolyn put forth a suggestion.

"Why don't you move back into your own room here?" she asked reasonably.

"But of course, that's the perfect solution," Paul concurred briskly.

"No." Peter's sharp tone conveyed exactly how unpalatable he found the suggestion. "There is no reason for Nicole to move out of the house." Peter was immediately bombarded from three sides with varied and personal arguments.

"I don't want to cramp your style," Nicole insisted around a knowing grin when Peter had maintained a stoic silence through the heated furor.

"There's little danger of that," Peter said. Then, afraid his sardonic tone revealed too much, he added smoothly, "The house is large enough to afford privacy to the three of us."

"But I want her here with me!" Carolyn persisted.

The glance Peter spared his mother was cutting with dismissal. "Nicole will stay with Patricia and me until she is ready to maintain her own place."

Carolyn appeared to grow an inch as she stiffened. "And if your *bride* objects?" she snapped.

"She won't." Peter's smile conveyed supreme confidence.

"But, Patricia, how can you possibly object?" Margaret demanded impatiently. "Certainly you realized you would have to meet Peter's family before the wedding?"

"Why?" Patricia turned from the window to gaze coolly at her mother. "The marriage is nothing but a farce."

"But they don't know that!" Margaret exclaimed. "And they're not to know it." Too upset to sit still, she sprang from the chair facing the desk. "Besides which," she continued as she paced from the chair to the wet bar in the corner, "I can't imagine Peter Vanzant living a farce."

An apprehensive chill feathered Patricia's spine. "What do you mean?" she asked, even though she was afraid she knew the answer.

Margaret came to an abrupt halt to stare at her daughter. "You know precisely what I mean. Peter is extremely attractive and, from all accounts, he is *extremely* virile as well!"

Patricia's eyes took on the look of gray glaciers. "Ours is to be a marriage of convenience," she said coldly.

"And Peter has a right to believe that a measure of that convenience will be the assuagement of his physical needs," Margaret said, her tone sharpening with growing impatience.

Her expression frozen, Patricia strode to the desk and grasped the phone.

"What in the world are you doing?" Margaret exploded, losing her legendary cool.

"I'm going to call off the marriage," Patricia said grimly, not bothering to glance at her mother.

"But why?" Margaret wailed, rushing to the desk to press the disconnect button with a trembling finger.

Patricia glared at Margaret. "I am not sleeping with Peter Vanzant," she hissed furiously.

"But, Patricia—" Margaret began in a reasonable tone.

"There are no buts." Patricia cut her off coldly. "My decision is final. Now, please remove your hand."

Margaret gave her a helpless look, but kept her finger firmly on the button. "Didn't you and Peter discuss the terms of agreement?" Margaret asked wearily.

Patricia smothered a groan of dismay. What kind of businesswoman was she? She *never* went to contract without scrutinizing terms! An empty sensation expanding inside, Patricia raised her head to meet her mother's questioning look.

"Well?" Margaret's tone chided, indicating she knew the answer. "You didn't discuss terms, did you?"

"No." Patricia's tone was defrosting rapidly.

Margaret frowned. "And now you're prepared to compound your error?"

Patricia's expression reflected her mother's. "What do you mean?"

"You are determined to contact Peter and cancel the agreement—is that correct?"

"Yes."

Margaret nodded and sighed. "Which is the same as breaking your word," she went on softly. "Is that not also correct?"

Patricia ached to argue the point—but could not. What her mother said was true. Verbal or written, an agreement was an agreement. If she refused to honor the commitment now, it *would* be a breach of her word. And Patricia had earned a reputation for being a woman of her word.

Reluctance evident in her slow movements, she carefully replaced the receiver. She would make her position clear as to sleeping arrangements *after* the ceremony. But, for now, Patricia knew she had no choice but to honor her word.

"You'll go through with it as agreed?" Margaret asked hesitantly.

"Yes."

"And you'll come to dinner to meet Peter's family?" She returned to the original subject.

Rebellion flared momentarily in Patricia's eyes, then the flame was banked, leaving her gray gaze as cool as usual. "Yes."

"Good." Margaret didn't attempt to hide the satisfaction she was feeling. "I expect the Vanzants at seven-thirty," she said, swinging away to head for the door. "I'm sure Peter will be in touch sometime this afternoon."

I can't wait. Patricia refrained from uttering the sarcastic comment. Anger abrading her emotions, she sat down at her desk and tried to concentrate on the requisitions she'd been working on when her mother had invaded her office. But, no matter how she reworked the figures, the fact remained that the need for supplies for one of her departments far exceeded the amount budgeted for them.

Was it possible, she asked herself, for even the much-vaunted Peter Vanzant to steer the company back to a financially viable position?

The much-vaunted Peter Vanzant chose that moment to ring her private number.

"Your mother has informed you about dinner tonight?" he said by way of greeting.

Patricia favored the telephone receiver with a dry look. "Yes." Her tone was even drier. "She said your family should arrive around seven-thirty."

"That's right." If Peter noted her tone, he gave no indication. "I think it would be wise if you and I arrived earlier. Do you agree?"

Would it matter? Patricia managed to keep the retort inside her mind. She also managed a neutral tone. "If you consider it necessary."

There was a very slight pause, then Peter responded briskly. "I do. There are a few points I think we must discuss."

Now he thinks we should have a discussion! Though Patricia's lips tightened, it didn't alter the tone of her voice. "Whatever you say. What time would you like me to be ready?"

"Would six-thirty be convenient?"

Patricia found she was swiftly coming to detest the word *convenient.* However, she answered him civilly. "Yes, of course."

It was not until after she'd hung up the phone that Patricia thought to wonder if Peter even knew where she lived. She certainly hadn't the vaguest idea what his address might be. Shrugging, she went back to work. Finding her was his problem.

Peter found her. Patricia's apartment doorbell rang at exactly six-twenty-seven.

Decked out to annihilate in a figure-hugging peacock-blue sheath, Patricia swung the door open and experienced the strangest sensation of having all the air leave her body.

Unquestionably handsome at any time, in evening attire Peter Vanzant was an assault to the female senses. His midnight-blue tuxedo underscored the darkness of his neatly brushed hair, his naturally dark skin and his glittering eyes. And, in stark contrast to all that darkness, his white ruffled shirt gleamed like a beacon in the night. On any other man, the starched ruffles might have lent an effeminate effect. But, on Peter, the narrow ruffles merely intensified his maleness. To say Peter Vanzant looked devastating would have been an understatement bordering on criminal.

Uncomfortable as everything feminine in her responded to everything masculine in him, Patricia raised her chin imperiously and stepped back automatically...as if removing herself from harm's way.

"Please, come in," Patricia said. The inflectionless tone of her voice had been hard fought for. "Can I get you a drink?"

"Yes. Thank you." As both his face and voice were equally devoid of expression, Patricia had no way of knowing how deeply moved Peter was by her appearance.

And Peter was affected, uncomfortably so. As he followed Patricia into the large, square living room, he absently noted the traditional decor in cool shades of pale blue and silvery gray. Yet as he noticed and approved her taste, his remote gaze inventoried her person.

In that instant Peter wanted her with every male impulse in his body. Unprepared for it, the jolt of physical desire stunned him into momentary immobility. He ached . . . everywhere.

"Scotch, isn't it?"

Oddly, the very coolness of Patricia's voice intensified the heat searing his bloodstream. Nodding, Peter inhaled slowly, and immediately knew he'd made a mistake. The combined scent of teasing perfume and tantalizing woman sent his senses reeling.

Striving to appear casual, he sank into the silvery depths of a plushly upholstered easy chair. Observing her as she approached him, glass in hand, Peter fought the urge to grasp her around her small waist and draw her onto his tautened thighs.

Damn! The harsh curse rang in Peter's head as he felt each tiny hair on the back of his hand quivering in response to the brief brush of her fingers against his as she handed him the glass.

"Not joining me?" One winged eyebrow arched as Peter raised the glass to gulp at the fiery whiskey.

"I think not." Patricia's lips tilted in a parody of a smile. "Except for the occasional glass of white wine, I seldom drink." Sitting down on the very edge of the matching chair facing his, she watched as Peter took a second deep swallow from the glass. Consternation drew a faint frown line between her delicately penciled eyebrows. "Do you drink a lot?" she asked, excusing her bluntness by deciding she had a right to know about his bad habits before the legal knot was irrevocably tied.

"No." A smile tugged at Peter's firm mouth as he shook his head. As his blood cooled, his mind sharpened. "We don't know each other at all, do we?" As he waited for her response, he was content to now sip at the Scotch remaining in the glass.

"Not at all," Patricia echoed.

"Yet, in less than a week, we'll be man and wife." Eyes narrowed, Peter watched her cheeks grow pale and her spine grow stiff. An inexplicable spasm of alarm roughened his tone. "Won't we?"

Beginning to feel cornered again, Patricia sliced a glance at the door, then back to his implacable expression. In an unusual display of nervousness, she wet her suddenly parched lips with the tip of her tongue. A sensation not unlike liquid fire poured through her body as his gaze clung to her parted lips.

He wanted to kiss her! The realization set her pulses hammering and her mind spinning. A sudden onslaught of sensual excitement was a shock to Patricia's entire nervous system. Her heartbeat accelerated, her breathing grew shallow and, unbelievably, she ached with the need to feel his hard mouth devouring hers.

She wanted to kiss him! Years of self-denial were wiped out in a flash of blinding desire to yield the softness of her mouth and body to the strength of his. Patricia began to tremble as long moments of silence stretched between them. And, in those moments, Peter's eyes, gleaming from behind his narrowed lids, spoke eloquently of the pleasure awaiting them with the merging of their bodies, one into the other.

Transfixed, Patricia stared into the dark depths of Peter's eyes, and felt the very foundation of her beliefs, of her life, begin to crumble.

No! The voice of self-preservation screamed inside her mind. *No. No.* She could not, would not, toss aside all the years of accumulated distrust and contempt she felt for the male of the species. In near desperation, Patricia forced the image of her father to the forefront of her consciousness.

The forming vision of the physically attractive, womanizing Alfred Lycaster proved the antidote to Patricia's sensual malady. Growing stronger by the second, Patricia managed to control the tremor in her fingers and the fire in her body by smothering both with a layer of ice.

Composed, withdrawn, Patricia met the flame of glittering desire in Peter's eyes and deflected it with a glacier-gray stare.

Peter felt the chilling look to the very heart of his masculinity. What the hell had happened? For an instant there, he would have sworn Patricia was his for the taking. His movements uncharacteristically awkward, Peter downed the last of the whiskey. Feeling rebuffed, and strangely insulted, he ran a weighing gaze over her frigid expression.

Something had turned Patricia off. Some memory, perhaps? As he pondered the possibility, determination hardened in Peter. Regardless

of what had turned her off, Peter vowed he'd
turn her on again. Maybe not tonight, and
maybe not tomorrow, but soon. He *would* have
her for his wife—in every definition of the word.

Four

Once again the tension fairly hummed through the air in the quiet room. Fighting an urge to squirm on the chair, Patricia managed to control her breathing process—which seemed to want to increase to a rapid puff-puff. Throughout the yawning silence, she had the distinct impression Peter was fighting a strong desire—not to make love to her but to throttle her!

"You said there were some matters we had to discuss before going to mother's," she reminded him, amazed at the steadiness of her tone.

"Um, my family," Peter murmured, as he leaned back in his chair. "The situation needs explaining." He met her cool stare head-on.

"Situation?" Patricia prompted when he fell silent.

"My mother is a bitch," Peter said without a trace of inflection. A cynical twist lifted his lips. "I thought it fair to warn you."

How considerate. Patricia kept the retort to herself, and questioned his statement by arching one neat eyebrow.

"She has a tendency to strike at me verbally," he went on in that deep, dark voice, "and her tongue is very sharp."

"I see," Patricia said, but of course she didn't, and he was well aware of it.

"I seriously doubt it." Peter's lips curved wryly. "But you will. And, when she strikes, I retaliate. It usually gets uncomfortable. And it always upsets my sister, Nicole."

"You have a sister?" Patricia's tone betrayed surprise. "I didn't know."

"How could you?" Peter shrugged. "As I said, we know practically nothing about each other. But, yes, I do have one sister." He hesitated, just long enough for a glint of challenge to brighten his eyes. "She lives with me, and I'd like her to continue to do so—'' his tone hardened a fraction ''—if you don't mind?''

Patricia knew very well that it wouldn't matter a rip if she minded his sister's presence or not. She allowed her expression to reveal her thoughts, but gave him the assurance he was demanding. ''No, I don't mind.'' However, she did expect some clarification. ''Is there a reason your sister lives with you?'' She moved her hand in a vague gesture. ''I mean, as opposed to living on her own or with your parents?'' For herself, Patricia couldn't imagine living in another person's home. In fact, she was experiencing some difficulty envisioning sharing a residence with Peter.

''There's always a reason, Patricia,'' Peter chided softly.

A chill snaked down Patricia's spine at the sound of her name on his lips, and she had to drag her attention back to what he was saying as he gave her a brief account of Nicole's accident and subsequent withdrawal.

''She's been living in my house for six months now,'' he concluded. ''And I don't want her to feel pressured about moving until she's ready.''

''No, of course not.'' Patricia felt an aching compassion for the young woman she had yet to meet. "Is she working, doing anything at all?" she asked softly, unconsciously revealing her own belief in the theory of occupation being the best medicine for Nicole's type of malady.

"No." Peter frowned. "At least, not as far as I know." A rueful smile shadowed his lips. "My consultancy business has kept me in New York for the most part."

Moving so swiftly he startled her, Peter got to his feet and strode to the liquor cabinet. "May I?" He held the bottle of Scotch aloft. At her nod he splashed the amber liquid into the glass, then turned to face her, a contemplative frown drawing a line between his brows.

"Nicole returned only yesterday from a two-week stay in New York City. I assumed she was visiting friends she hadn't seen since the accident." His eyes narrowed with his thoughts. "But now, I wonder if she might have been looking for work."

"And would it bother you if she had been looking?" Patricia asked, reading his expression correctly.

The frown furrow deepened above the bridge of Peter's nose. "I'm not sure if she's emotionally ready to go back to work," he said roughly, defensively.

"And I feel sure that, if she's looking, she's ready," Patricia countered. For a moment, the very self-assured, often arrogant Peter Vanzant looked helpless and uncertain. For the length of that moment, Patricia felt a kernel of undesired, unwanted kinship for him. Allowing an impulse to dictate her actions, she rose and walked to him. Placing her hand on his arm, she curled and tightened her fingers in a reassuring squeeze.

"Your sister must work her way back in her own time, by her own methods." Her usually cool tone had given way to earnestness. "The only way we can help is by being there if and when she needs us." Intent on easing his strain, Patricia didn't even notice her use of the words *we* and *us*.

Peter noticed. He also noticed other things, noticed and responded to them. Tenderness swelled in his chest at her offer of assistance. Surprise sharpened his glance at her face, made more beautiful than ever by compassion. Heat rushed through his body from the one point of contact where her palm lay on his arm.

His gaze lowered to that slender, delicately formed hand, burning the flesh of his forearm through the material of his shirt and suit coat. Her gaze followed his. For one instant they were joined, one to the other, physically, mentally, silently admitting to a need for human contact. And something happened to both—a softening in him, a melting in her—although it would be a long time before either would admit it to the other.

For the present, Peter savored the offer of her strength aligned with his, and responded to the fire licking through his veins. Slowly, dreamlike, he raised his hand and covered hers, in a symbolic gesture of gratitude and sheer male possession.

The gesture pierced Patricia's near mesmeric state. Floundering in emotions alien and unsettling, she grasped at normalcy in the form of the slim watch circling her wrist.

"It—it's seven-fifteen!" she gasped around the dry ache in her throat. "Hadn't we better leave for mother's?"

After the strange, intimate interlude in her apartment, dinner seemed rather mundane to Patricia, even with the occasional, if sweetly delivered, sarcastic remark from Carolyn Vanzant.

More than ever on guard, her icy composure firmly intact, Patricia found it almost ludicrously easy to deflect Carolyn's politely phrased put-downs. By the time Margaret's maid removed the soup course it was obvious to everyone present that, should push ever come to shove between the two strikingly beautiful women, the older of the two wouldn't stand a chance. Though acid-tongued, Carolyn was all cotton-candy fluff. By comparison, though soft-spoken, Patricia was solid steel coated with frost.

Paul Vanzant was a different story. Patricia discovered she liked Peter's father midway between introductions and the announcement that dinner was served.

Urbane, good-looking, businesslike even in relaxation, Paul typified everything Patricia's own father had sorely lacked. Like his son, Paul was sharp of eye and soft of voice, most especially when he spoke to Nicole.

And Nicole was in a class all by herself. Patricia made the judgment about her future sister-in-law on sight. As the evening progressed, she decided her first impression, as usual, was correct.

Nicole was not merely beautiful. There was something about her that transcended the accepted definition of beauty. Searching for words, Patricia came up with ethereal, enchanting, symmetrical perfection of features, all of which applied, but were nevertheless inadequate.

By itself, Nicole's beauty would not have impressed Patricia. But she quickly realized there was much more to the former model than surface loveliness.

Like her brother, Nicole was tall with dark hair and eyes, but there the similarities ended. Where Peter projected an image of strength, self-assurance and sheer male arrogance, Nicole gave the impression of retiring gentleness and exquisite fragility.

Her dark eyes glowed with warmth, her voice was soft, her rare laughter a light caress on the ears of her listeners. Captivated, Patricia observed Nicole throughout the meal and, long before dessert and champagne were served, reached the conclusion that she could happily share her husband's house with Nicole. It was sharing the house with Peter that bothered Patricia.

Carolyn's few snide remarks aside, the entire evening proved a smashing success for Margaret. After the elder Vanzants departed, offering to drop Nicole at Peter's house on the way, Margaret fixed final drinks for Patricia, Peter and herself. Lifting her glass aloft, she proposed a not-altogether-teasing toast.

"To the merger," she said in satisfied tones, "and the continued success of two prominent

Philadelphia families." A devilish twinkle lit her eyes from within as she added, innocently, "Long may they prosper and grow."

Peter's lips slanted wryly, but he tossed back his drink, emptying his glass.

Patricia's gray eyes clouded, but she sipped daintily at the pale gold wine.

Observing them from beneath lowered lids, Margaret smiled in secret contentment.

As D day approached—in Patricia's mind, D standing for "doom"; hers—Patricia had the oddest sensation of having stumbled into a surrealistic world, which was certainly not of her own making.

Her secretary, Donna, simpered all over the office like some flighty Regency heroine. The other female employees in the departments under Patricia's management smiled mistily at her whenever she made an appearance, and sighed longingly on the occasions Peter strode through the offices. Margaret was as high, and just about as dependable, as a lush on a three-day bender. Even the security man at Patricia's apartment seemed to trip all over himself in his rush to open doors or flag cabs for her. But the most astonishing reaction to the announcement of Patricia's marriage to Peter came from the dour-faced members of the board of directors who, one by one, deserted their various, and in Patricia's opinion, probably nefarious, pursuits to pay her personal visits to offer congratulations. Surrealistic indeed!

Patricia, clinging to sanity in an atmosphere more bubbly than wedding champagne, went about her business as usual, at least as much as possible. With brisk practicality, she shopped for a dress and accessories suitable for a marriage of the arranged variety. At the last minute, panic threatened to overwhelm her. Sheer willpower kept Patricia's body upright and her hand steady as she repeated the sacred vows of marriage. With the exchange of rings, Patricia imagined she heard a door close behind her.

The lavish reception Peter had insisted upon was everything Patricia had feared it would be and worse.

Over three hundred of the very best people sat down to a dinner of prime roast beef in the ornate ballroom of the center city hotel. Everyone commented on how very delicious the meal was. Although she agreed with each and every one, Patricia had no way of knowing if the food was excellent or terrible, as she barely touched it. Patricia's stomach muscles were tightly clenched.

All the accepted rituals were performed. The bride and groom were toasted with champagne. The groom's hand steadied the bride's as the first slice was made into the multitiered cake. The feted couple took the polished floor for the traditional first dance. Both the bride and groom smiled—brilliantly and often. Patricia was positive her face would crack.

The dance band hired for the occasion rendered both modern up-tempo and sentimental standards, one after the other, on and on and on. The beat throbbed inside Patricia's head.

After an hour the ivory-toned, brocaded suit she had chosen to be married in began to weigh like a suit of armor on Patricia's shoulders. The gold-shot, raw-silk blouse she wore with the suit clung in patches to her perspiration-dewed body. The high, narrow heels on the dainty, ivory-tinted shoes she wore were a choice she ruefully regretted. Patricia's feet hurt.

Yet, through it all, Patricia glided like a shimmering slender reed. Her shoulders were back, her smile was in place and one hand rested on the smooth material covering her husband's muscular forearm as they drifted from one laughing group to another to receive the best wishes gushingly proffered by their guests. And, through it all, Patricia's carefully concealed irritation was continuously abraded by the groom's apparent enjoyment of the celebratory party.

Which only proved how deceiving appearances could be.

Facial muscles aching from being forced into an upward tilt, Peter guided his bride around the spacious ballroom and wished he was at home. As parties went, the reception was a good one. But Peter hated parties.

The silver-gray suit outlining his tall, broad-shouldered frame to advantage, and contrasting effectively with his dark good looks, had not come off a rack but had been tailored to perfection. The pristine white silk shirt and gray and muted red-striped tie complementing the suit both bore a discreetly hidden designer label. Peter felt smothered by the fine fabric and strangled by the neck gear.

The champagne bubbling merrily in the fluted glass he held had been imported from France and purchased by the case. Peter longed for three fingers of aged Scotch undiluted by ice or water.

As one long hour was followed by another even longer hour, Peter found himself wondering what in hell he was doing, socializing in the middle of the afternoon with people he didn't particularly care about. At odd moments, his glance was captured by the glint of gold sparked from the blazing crystal chandeliers overhead and bouncing off the symbolic rings circling the finger on the hand resting on his arm, or the one on the hand clutching the fragile glass. Peter was hard-pressed to keep from grasping Patricia's hand and bolting through the nearest exit.

When the outer edge of patience was reached, Peter bent protectively, caringly over Patricia and whispered close to her ear.

"What do you say we blow this joint, honey?"

At the sound of his low, insinuating tone and his phrasing, Patricia went as stiff as a salted cod. Then she began to tremble from the force of the battle being waged inside between her sense of propriety and the laughter rising in her throat. Fortunately, amusement won the short-lived struggle. Turning her head, she felt a surprising but delicious shock as her lips lightly brushed his earlobe.

"I—ah—I need to visit the ladies' room first," she murmured, echoing his conspiratorial tone.

"Okay." He paused, considering, then instructed, "You go out one way and I'll saunter out another." His warm, moist breath whispered into her ear and Patricia felt it tingle all the way to her aching feet. "I'll meet you at the side entrance in, say... ten minutes?"

"Yes, ten minutes," Patricia breathed. Stepping back, she smiled brilliantly for all who happened to be observing them, then set off determinedly for the exit.

A few minutes later, Patricia walked out of the ladies' room and calmly turned in the direction away from the ballroom. Her stride long but unhurried, she moved along the wide corridor that led to the hotel's side entrance. Her steps faltered when she heard the murmur of voices, one vaguely familiar, coming from an alcove ahead and to the right of her. As she drew alongside the alcove, Patricia casually glanced at the couple hidden within its shadowy depths. Gray eyes widening in shock, Patricia came to a dead stop.

Carolyn Vanzant, Peter's *mother*, was locked in a passionate embrace with a man Peter had introduced to Patricia as one of his friends from childhood. The attractive man was Peter's age, possibly a year or two younger!

Patricia paused only an instant before hastening on, yet during that infinitesimal hesitation, she had clearly witnessed the couple's hungry kiss.

Peter's mother. *Her* mother-in-law! Shaken, Patricia approached the side entrance with trepidation. Peter was outside, waiting for her. She could see the sparkle of sunlight reflecting off of his gleaming burgundy Mercedes. What in heaven's name could she say to him? For a second she felt physically sick.

Nothing. Say nothing about what you saw, Patricia advised herself firmly. *This is a* convenience *marriage. If there's a problem or problems in Peter's family, they are* their *problems—not* yours.

Composing herself, Patricia pushed through the wide door. For a moment, her heart ached for the man leaning indolently against the shiny proof of wealth. Peter's usually austere expression had given way to a look endearingly similar to that of a tricky young boy playing hooky from school.

Lord, she is beautiful! And she's my wife! The thoughts stirred the desire that had been simmering inside Peter into a clawing ache. As Patricia crossed the sidewalk to him, Peter straightened and swung the passenger door open for her. Anxious to get home, he circled the driver's side and slid behind the wheel.

"We've escaped," he drawled, easing the car into the late-afternoon traffic.

"And without having to endure the fuss of the ritualistic rice pelting." Patricia sighed her relief.

Like a pinprick deflates a balloon, Patricia's dry observation drained all the buoyancy from Peter. Suddenly he felt extremely tired, and on the verge of bad temper.

"All things considered," he said, in a deceptively mild tone, "everything went well."

"I suppose," Patricia responded absently.

Her indifference sent a shaft of sheer fury crackling through Peter's body. Damn it! he fumed, gripping the wheel in a stranglehold. Anticipating this evening, he'd lived through a hell of wanting her all week. The fantasies he'd concocted during the long sleepless nights had imbued that anticipation with sweet anguish. Now, with the moment of blessed relief mere miles away, his *bride* offered him indifference!

Preventing a groan by gritting his teeth, Peter drove those remaining miles in angry silence. By the time he parked the car in the driveway of his suburban town house, his insides felt like a caldron, bubbling with raging anger and sexual frustration.

"I think I'll take a short bath and a long nap."

Patricia's cool comment as they entered the flagstone foyer did not bank the fire roaring in Peter's mind and body. Her touch-me-not attitude didn't help much, either.

"My housekeeper left a tray of delicacies for our supper," Peter carefully informed her, in a too-soft, warning tone.

Though Patricia noticed the tension in his voice, she chose to ignore it. "It'll keep." She tossed the comment over her shoulder carelessly, heading with determination toward the broad, open staircase. She had reached the next to the last step to the second-floor landing when Peter's voice stopped her.

"I'll change and join you with a drink in a few minutes."

It was at that point that Patricia was attacked by a bad case of the shakes. Visibly trembling, she forced her legs to carry her the short distance to the bedroom she'd claimed for herself the previous week when she'd come to the house for the purpose of transferring her clothes.

Originally planned as a nursery, the bedroom was connected to the master bedroom—Peter's room. The suite included a large bathroom, accessible to both bedrooms. Threads of panic were working a drawstring effect on Patricia's throat as she rushed into the room. Closing and locking the door behind her, she slumped against the solid panel, breathing deeply. As a measure of calm returned, Patricia sent her gaze skimming over the interior of the adequate-sized room.

The plush carpet was in a honey-gold shade, complementing the rich patina of the one wall paneled in dark walnut. The remaining three walls were covered with grass-fiber paper in a muted green. The draperies and bedspread were a deep forest green, as were the cushions on the wicker lounge chair by the single oversize window. All the other furniture in the room was constructed of wicker and painted a gleaming white. A large Boston fern trailed lacy leaves from a white pot nestled in a braided hanger.

Patricia had fallen in love with the room at first sight, even though it had a door, now shut, that led to the master bedroom. Eyeing the door warily, Patricia straightened and walked to it, turning the lock decisively. Knowing she was safely locked in eased the tension eating at her nerves. A sigh of relief whispering through her lips, she dropped her tiny, useless purse onto the lounger and shrugged out of her suit jacket.

Some twenty minutes later, her body covered by a mid-thigh-length wraparound, Patricia firmly locked the bathroom door before running the bathwater. When, finally, she slid her tired body into the silky water that nearly filled the extra-long, extra-deep black-marble tub, Patricia softly moaned her pleasure aloud.

"If it feels that good perhaps I should join you in there."

Her moan of pleasure changing to a groan of dismay, Patricia slowly turned to the possessor of that low, sexy voice. Pride forbade the maidenly act of attempting to hide herself with splayed hands. Anger dictated the frost that sheened the gray eyes studying him disdainfully.

In actual fact, there was precious little about Peter's appearance to disdain. In a word, he looked exciting, attired in nothing but a short silver-gray robe in a silky material. His dark hair, though neatly brushed, seemed intent on slipping onto his forehead and the taut skin on his cheeks gleamed from contact with a sharp razor blade. His spicy after-shave wafted on the steamy air to tickle Patricia's senses. The bottle of champagne and two glasses he was holding, and the slumberous gleam in his eyes, proclaimed his intention of seduction.

"Be my guest." Standing swiftly, Patricia plucked a towel from the rack on the wall, concealing her curvaceous body in its folds. Appearing calm was costing her dearly in nerves, which seemed intent on jumping out of her skin. Stepping onto the checkered black and white carpet, she indicated the tub with a sweep of one hand. "It's all yours," she said. Her carriage that of a queen, Patricia swept into her bedroom.

Peter's soft, appreciative laughter followed her. So did he. Her back to him, Patricia gritted her teeth but stood tall as she discarded the towel and slid her silky nightgown over her head. She turned to face him, eyebrows raised, as she drew on the matching peignoir.

"Is this not *my* room?" she asked haughtily.

"Are you not *my* wife?" he retorted in kind.

Patricia frowned. "Technically, yes."

Peter laughed. "Technically, legally and permanently." His laughter faded. His eyes narrowed. "Do you understand?"

Patricia fought the urge to clutch the peignoir closer to her breasts. She was helpless against the rapid beat of her heart and shallowness of her breath. Feeling trapped, she made a show of strolling to the bed to sit on the edge. In a bid to divert him, she attacked. "How did you get into the bathroom? I distinctly remember locking the door."

His action reflecting hers, Peter sauntered across the room to perch beside her. His shrug spoke eloquently. He spoke bluntly.

"I have a key." His eyes glittered. His smile taunted. "I own the house—remember?"

"And because the house is yours," she retaliated, "I'm to be allowed no privacy at all?" She leveled her most freezing stare at him. Peter didn't freeze, he fired up.

"Damn it, Patricia!" he exploded. "This is our wedding night!"

"I don't remember agreeing to spend this night, or any other night, with you!" Patricia's tone was defrosting with her own angry heat.

"I don't remember discussing *any* of the practical details of this marriage with you!" Peter's voice was one notch below a shout. The delicate, long-stemmed wineglasses rattled as he moved his hand impatiently.

Now Patricia fought the urge to sink her teeth into her bottom lip. Nervous apprehension was giving her tingling sensations all over her body; at least she *hoped* it was nervous apprehension. She was also suddenly very dry.

"Are you going to pour that wine or just wave the glasses around?" she snapped irritably.

Peter looked blank for an instant, then he frowned. "Do you want some?"

"Well, since it's open, we might as well drink it. Champagne's too expensive to simply let it go flat."

Peter grinned; he couldn't help it. Her tone was so exactly that of a practical, economic wife, he had no choice—it was either grin or curse.

"I don't believe this," he muttered, handing a glass to her before carefully pouring out the sparkling wine. "I really don't believe this."

"But you were quick to believe it when mother waved her shares of stock in front of you." Patricia was immediately sorry for the gibe, because it banished his grin and tightened his lips.

"That's right," he said in a deathly quiet tone. "And so were you." Raising his glass, he smiled sardonically. "Your health, *Mrs*. Vanzant. And to your future *as* Mrs. Vanzant."

Patricia hesitated, trying to decide whether to honor his toast or not. But then his eyes narrowed and glittered with intent. He was spoiling for a fight, she knew it, and suddenly she feared it. Gathering every ounce of willpower she possessed, she raised her glass and smiled.

"*Your* health, *Mr.* Vanzant," she mimicked mockingly.

Five

The wine was cool on her tongue and parched throat. Patricia drank thirstily, draining the glass. Peter refilled the glass as she lowered it from her lips.

"For a woman who claims she rarely drinks," he observed in a tone as dry as the wine, "you knocked that back pretty neatly."

"It's been a long, exhausting day," Patricia defended herself. "I'm very tired," she added, pointedly. "I was hoping for a nap."

"I'm sorry, but the nap will have to wait." Peter didn't sound in the least sorry. "We have got some serious talking to do.'' She opened her mouth to protest. ''Now,'' he added, forestalling her.

Patricia's shoulders ached with the need to slump wearily. She straightened her spine with grim determination. ''All right, we'll talk.'' She lifted the glass to her lips again, but this time she sipped at the wine daintily. Over the rim of the glass, she arched her brows promptingly.

Peter eyed her narrowly, sipping his own wine. When he spoke, it was with the same jarring bluntness he'd used earlier. ''Do you plan to honor your marriage vows?''

Startled, Patricia stammered. ''Wh—what do you—ah—mean?'' She drew a breath, then clarified. ''In what way?''

''In *every* way,'' Peter retorted. ''But first, do you intend to honor the vow of fidelity?''

A strange, unusual phenomenon occurred in Patricia; she blushed. She also took exception to his question.

''Yes! Certainly!'' she exclaimed.

''And do you expect me to honor the same vow?'' he persisted.

Rattled by having her morals questioned, Patricia didn't recognize the trap. She stepped blindly into it. ''I would hope so!'' An image of his mother—his *unfaithful* mother—sprang into her mind. Her lips curved cynically. "Had you thought I wouldn't expect you to honor it?"

The slant of his lips mirrored hers. Draining his glass, Peter set it on the floor before responding. "To tell you the absolute truth, Patricia, I don't know what the hell to think about this whole crazy arrangement." Reaching out, he took the glass from her hand and set it next to his. "You've as much as told me that you have no intention of sleeping with me." His lips moved in a parody of a smile . . . an unpleasant smile. "Is that correct?"

Though Patricia had to swallow to moisten her dry throat, when she answered, her voice was firm. "Yes."

"Yeah," he grunted around a tired-sounding chuckle. "Yet you expect me to remain faithful. Curious." One dark eyebrow arched. "Do you have any suggestions as to how I'm supposed to manage that?"

Patricia had no answer. What answer was there, other than the obvious one? "No." Her icy tone had melted to a thin trickle.

She was pulling away. Peter could actually see her withdrawing into herself. *Damn, what is with this woman?* he railed silently, trying to control the frustration and impatience that threatened to overcome his good sense. Patricia *had* agreed to the arrangement. She was here, in his house, wearing nothing but a gown and peignoir, which left little to the imagination and were playing hell with his libido. He was here, his silk robe the only barrier between her gaze and his obvious arousal. They were husband and wife. What would be more natural than to consummate the vows they had exchanged?

Besides which, Peter ached for her, ached in a way so intense and painful it baffled him. Yet a voice deep inside warned against insistence. But, even without the instinctive warning, Peter rebelled against instigating force. He had never forced compliance from any woman and he certainly wasn't about to start with his wife! He wanted her, badly, but he wanted her soft and willing. At that moment, Patricia was neither.

Tentatively, testingly, Peter raised his hand to lightly brush her pale cheek with his fingertips. Patricia made no protest, but she did flinch. Swallowing the urge to sigh, and the need to curse, Peter slowly withdrew his hand.

"I'm a normal, healthy man, Patricia."

His even tone reverberated inside Patricia's head. Chilled except for the fiery trail left by the brush of his fingers on her cheek, she stared at Peter and engaged in a silent battle with her conscience.

Denying him is cheating, her conscience nagged.

I can't surrender, her pride insisted.

In all fairness, you must, her conscience jabbed.

I'll think about it, her pride hedged.

"I need time," Patricia murmured aloud, ending the silent inner war.

Peter's expression assumed the austerity she was accustomed to. "How much time?" he asked tonelessly.

"I—I don't know." Patricia swallowed around the lump in her throat.

"You don't know," Peter repeated, his tone mocking. A cynical smile twisting his lips, he gathered up the bottle of wine and the glasses. Rising as if it hurt him, he walked to the door connecting the two rooms. His hand on the ornate knob, he turned to stare at her with eyes devoid of feeling. His voice was hard, taunting, insulting.

"How were you planning to let me know?" he wondered aloud, then answered the question for her. "By waving a white teddy to indicate your surrender?"

Aware that he had every reason for his expectations, and smarting under the stinging darts from her conscience, Patricia had been softening, her inner core of ice melting. His deliberate crudity offended her, hardening her will again. Her eyes turned glacial.

"It will be a cold day—" she began.

"Don't bother, I get the picture." Peter cut her off, his action betraying his agitation as he pulled the door open. Then, adding injury to insult, he sniped, "I don't know if I'd derive enjoyment from making love to an ice sculpture anyway."

Incensed, Patricia retaliated without consideration. "You can always follow your mother's example."

Peter went dead still then, slowly, he turned to face her, his harsh expression frightening. His dark eyes glittered with fury. "What do you know about my mother?" His voice sent a chill of apprehension up Patricia's spine.

"Nothing, not really." Fully aware of being in the wrong, Patricia had to steel herself to meet his stare. "I'm—I'm sorry. I had no right—" Again he interrupted her.

"That's correct," he snapped. "And, until the day you are truly my wife, your only rights in *my* house are those of any other guest."

She deserved his tone of utter disgust, yet defiance flared in Patricia. Rising from the edge of the bed, she walked to him, one hand extended.

"In that case," she said coldly, "as a guest in *your* house, I'd like the key to the door, *please*."

"There will be no locked doors between us, Patricia." His remote gaze swept over her slender form. "But don't worry, you needn't lay trembling in your cold bed in fear of me. I will come and go as I please in my own home, but I do *not* stoop to violation—" his lips twitched "—of wife or guest." Very gently, he closed the door in her face.

On either side of an unlocked door, both Peter and Patricia spent the sleepless night wrestling with their respective consciences and personal devils. And, inside each, self-acknowledgment waxed as anger waned.

To Patricia's consternation, her bed did feel cold—cold and unwelcoming. Still reeling from his rapier-sharp tongue-lashing, she was further surprised by a strong desire to cry, and Patricia hadn't cried since her fifteenth year.

Even as she assured herself that she would not cry, especially over a beast like Peter, hot tears trickled from her eyes. Brushing her fingers impatiently over her wet cheeks, she slid from the bed to pace the length and width of the dark room. In the midst of her pacing, Patricia felt oddly comforted by the muffled sounds from the room next to hers. Strangely, knowing that Peter was as restless as she eased the tension crawling along her nerves.

He had every right to expect her to share his bed.

The thought sprang into her mind as a measure of calm returned. Hadn't her mother said as much? Patricia acknowledged that she had indeed been forewarned. Yet, in her arrogance, she had convinced herself of her ability to handle Peter.

A mirthless laugh whispered through her dry lips. How naive could a supposedly bright, twenty-eight-year-old woman be? In her all-consuming desire for control of the company, she had entered into an agreement without first thinking through all the possible ramifications. Her mother had warned her of Peter's reputation as a very virile man. And hadn't she seen the proof of his arousal with her own eyes?

A shudder ripped through her body with unexpected violence. Patricia knew she really had little choice. Unless she ended the marriage immediately, she would eventually have to share his bed. But, God, how could she, feeling as she did about men?

Patricia's contempt for the male of the species had begun the winter she had turned fifteen. Arriving home early one Friday afternoon from the private school she'd attended, she had tossed her coat and books onto a chair, then dashed up the stairs to the second floor of the three-storied house her mother's family had occupied for three generations. Patricia had been searching for her mother to ask permission to go shopping with a friend. She hadn't found her mother, who, she later learned, was playing in a bridge tournament. But Patricia had found her father.

To avoid being chastised for unladylike haste, Patricia had slowed her headlong dash into a sedate walk before she had reached her parents' bedroom. Circumspectly, she had knocked lightly on the door before turning the knob and entering. The door opened silently on well-oiled hinges. The scene that met her eyes shattered her halcyon existence and killed the love and respect she had for her father.

In the middle of the afternoon, her father was in the bedroom with a woman who was not his wife. Shocked into immobility, Patricia had stared in horror at the man and woman locked together in a passionate embrace. Neither had heard Patricia's light tap on the door.

Becoming sick to her stomach, Patricia ran for the bathroom, where she'd been violently ill.

Her eyes opened by the incident, Patricia quickly learned the extent of her father's infidelities. After some careful probing, Patricia was convinced that Margaret was innocently unaware of her husband's unfaithfulness. And so, in the desire to protect her mother, Patricia bore the knowledge of her father's philandering by herself.

But the seed of contempt had been planted. Then, in her second year of college, the seed sprouted, sending tenacious shoots to twine around every fiber of Patricia's being.

In her sophomore year of college, Patricia fell in love. And, like all young girls in the throes of first love, she regarded her beloved as perfect. He wasn't. Like many of his contemporaries, the object of Patricia's affections was merely scoring points. Since Patricia had a reputation as being not only hard, but impossible, to get, her point value was high. Finding out that she had yielded her virginity to enhance a man's ego had started the inner icing. Observing the sexual practices of others over the years had added layer upon layer of ice to Patricia's emotions.

And now, in her twenty-eighth year, Patricia found herself married to a veritable blowtorch.

Patricia paced the length and width of her dark room.

On the other side of the door, Peter prowled the larger bedroom, pausing at intervals to glare at the solid panel. He could hear her, sense her; she was so very near, and so very out of reach.

Frustration eating at his nerves relentlessly, he tore the robe off and flung himself onto the oversize, empty bed. Silently he lay, staring at the stark white ceiling.

It was his wedding night and he was ready—lord, was he ready—but his bride of less than twelve hours was as inaccessible to him as if she were on another planet!

How had he gotten himself into this stupid arrangement?

A derisive smile pulled at Peter's tight lips. It was almost funny. Almost? Ha! It was ludicrously funny! He was Peter Vanzant—a man who had vowed never to shackle himself to the whims of one woman. He, a man who had adroitly avoided pledging love to any woman, now lay in his own sweat of agony, while his *bride*, his own personal Lady Ice, was probably laughing herself silly in her sanctuary one door away.

It was enough to make a grown man weep.

A sigh expanding his broad chest, Peter glanced at the hand-carved door, then slowly closed his eyes. Was he being dealt retribution for past sins? Peter laughed, silently, hollowly. If he was now paying for previous transgressions, he was in for a long period of even longer nights.

The image of a young woman formed in his mind, vivid, clear, too clear. Peter winced. Was this how Barbara had felt? he wondered for the very first time.

Feeling a stab of guilt, Peter recalled the only woman he had ever lived with.

A model and a friend of Nicole's, Barbara had been the only woman to even come close to capturing Peter's heart. His conscience hurting, he remembered his satisfaction when she had agreed to move into his New York City apartment, and his triumph on discovering she was still a virgin. He had accepted her virginity, and her love, gratefully, but had given her only *things* in return, never anything of himself. And he'd even had the arrogant gall to be angry when she left him alone in his elegant cage.

Was this demeaning sense of cold rejection what Barbara had felt?

Reduced from exceptional man to human by a situation he had walked into with his eyes open, Peter honestly, if belatedly, hoped Barbara was happy with the Texas rancher she had married the previous fall.

With his eyes open. The phrase echoed inside Peter's head. Why had he accepted Margaret's proposition? He certainly didn't need the firm she'd offered him on a plate—along with her daughter. In addition to the fortune he had inherited from his maternal grandmother, Peter had made an amazing success of his consultancy business and, in all modesty, was well aware of being considered the best. So then, why walk into a company on the verge of going under?

His body now at ease, free of the aching tension, Peter opened his eyes to stare at the closed door. He knew the answers; he simply hadn't wanted to examine them.

Now, in retrospect, Peter remembered the amusement with which he'd received Margaret's proposal. And, although he had requested a look at the company's financial accounts, he had not seriously considered Margaret's offer. Not until he had walked into Patricia's office, and been presented with her back ... which had been as nothing compared to the challenge she'd posed when she'd turned to face him.

Patricia had looked magnificent. With a growing sense of wonder, Peter realized that on first sight he had wanted her for himself. His eyes narrowed as he contemplated the door. Had he, the man who had made exquisite love while never murmuring the words of love, fallen headlong into that most unstable of emotions at first sight? Peter shuddered and closed his eyes, and his mind, to speculation.

The night wore on. It wore on Patricia's nerves. It wore on Peter's conscience. It wore on relentlessly, until it finally wore itself out. The first pink streaks of dawn were greeted by soft sighs of relief from two weary individuals, separated by the chasm of an inch and a half of carved wood.

For Patricia, exhaustion had settled into numbness. Her body weighted, her eyes gritty, she prepared to escape the four walls she was beginning to feel were closing in on her. After splashing cold water on her face and brushing her teeth, she dressed casually in slacks and a silk knit sweater. Long past artifice, she left her face free of makeup. Assuming her usual brisk stride, she left the room and went to the kitchen, positive that the only way she'd be able to get through the day would be by fortifying herself with coffee—a lot of coffee.

She was standing by the kitchen counter, staring fixedly at the dark brew trickling into the glass container under the automatic coffee maker, when Peter ambled into the room. Although she hadn't heard his approach, Patricia knew the instant he hesitated in the doorway.

"Good morning." Patricia addressed the coffee maker. Tension tugged at her nerves as she waited for a response—or a lack of one.

"Good morning." Peter smiled wryly as he entered the room. Wondering if he were facing a future of speaking to her back, he walked to stand next to her at the counter, to join her in the fascinating pastime of watching the coffee as it dripped into the glass pot.

"Almost ready?" His smile turned dry. For appearances' sake, they had agreed to spend a week away from the office. At that moment, Peter envisioned an entire week of stilted conversation.

"Yes." Patricia scoured her mind for something to add and came up empty. The coming week stretched endlessly before her.

"Good." Peter frowned, searching for something to add. "I, ah, I think I'll see if the paper's here yet." He turned and headed for the door.

By the time Peter returned to the kitchen, without the paper, which had not yet been delivered, Patricia was sitting at the table, a delicate gold-rimmed cup cradled in her hands. A trail of steam rose from the matching cup she'd set at the place opposite her. As he slid onto the thickly padded, velour-covered chair, Peter mused that, although her gaze was lowered to her cup, he had gained a minor victory—at least he was facing her.

"Not hungry?" he asked, groaning silently. "I can rustle something up if you are," he went on before she could reply. "I scramble a mean egg." Inside, Peter was berating himself for giving his housekeeper the week off.

Patricia raised her head slowly. Peter almost wished she hadn't. Her eyes were cold, her expression remote.

"Please, don't feel you must cater to me." Patricia's voice sounded as if it came from the depths of a tomb, a very chilly tomb. "I am perfectly capable of preparing a meal." Despairing her tone, which came from tiredness more than disinterest, she offered him a hesitant smile. "As a matter of fact, I'm really a very good cook."

"Indeed?" Hoping he was reading her smile correctly, Peter injected a hint of teasing into his tone.

Taking the hint, Patricia smiled more easily. "Indeed," she mimicked. "Though I have a woman who comes in to clean, she does not cook for me. I prepare my own meals."

"You *had* a woman come in to clean," he clarified gently. "You live here now." Peter immediately regretted the flat-sounding statement. His breath eased through his lips when Patricia smiled wryly instead of coldly.

"Yes, but I've retained her until I decide what I'm going to do with the apartment," she informed him quietly.

"You own it?" The question brought home to Peter how very little they knew about each other.

"Yes," Patricia murmured, suddenly aware of how ignorant they were of each other's lives. She was also struck by the even more forceful realization that she had repeated vows of commitment to this stranger seated across the table from her.

Patricia felt utterly, unbelievably tired. The prospect of solving the dilemma she had blindly gotten herself into overwhelmed her. Was there any possible way she could share a future with this stranger who was her husband? she asked herself, swallowing a tide of renewed nervousness. Patricia hadn't a clue as to where to begin.

Fortunately, Peter did. Since his thoughts were similar to hers, Peter opted to begin with breakfast, and take it slowly and carefully from there. Pushing his chair back, he got to his feet.

"We both missed dinner last night, and I'm starving." He offered her his hand along with a smile. "Shall we see if we can dazzle each other with our culinary expertise?"

Grateful for the opening, Patricia placed her hand in his.

"What do you usually have for breakfast?" Peter asked absently, leading her to the refrigerator.

"Grapefruit juice, a poached egg and a slice of whole-wheat bread."

Drawing his head back from behind the refrigerator door, Peter ran a glance over her slim form. His look alone spoke volumes. "I hesitate to inquire what you eat for lunch and dinner," he drawled, returning his attention to the interior of the refrigerator.

"I seldom eat lunch," Patricia said. "And I usually broil a small steak or chop for dinner."

"Figures." Peter shook his head and shot her a dry look. "Well, I can live with the juice, egg and toast but, if you have no objections, I'll just jazz it up a bit."

Peter's way of jazzing up breakfast came in a can marked corned-beef hash, which he removed from a cabinet above the counter while Patricia set the table.

Surprisingly, they worked well together. Patricia poured the juice while Peter gathered the frying pan and three-egg poacher. Peter heated the hash while Patricia timed the eggs. He dropped the bread into the toaster; she buttered it when it popped up. When everything was ready they portioned it accordingly—one ladle of hash and one egg for Patricia, the remainder of the hash and two eggs for Peter. And, though they consumed the meal in relative silence, it was a comfortable silence, free of the strain and tension that had simmered between them earlier. To her amazement, Patricia decided she liked the hash, and told him so.

"It'll put a little meat on your bones," Peter teased, rising to carry their cups to the counter and refill them.

Patricia stiffened, then relaxed. The narrow-eyed way in which Peter was watching her indicated that he was waiting for a stinging response from her. Was she really so very uptight? she mused, holding his expectant gaze. So quick to take offense? Of course she was—hadn't she carefully cultivated the sprouting seed of contempt?

"But I have excellent bones," she rejoined, matching his teasing note. "Why hide them beneath a little meat?"

Peter laughed, freely, openly, and a strange thing happened. Patricia discovered she liked the sound of his laughter. Like his voice, his laughter was deep and rich and darkly exciting. It was also contagious. Patricia laughed with him. The expression that filled his face, for all its briefness, told her that he enjoyed the sound of her laughter as well.

"Point taken."

Peter made the comment in a bland, unrevealing tone. Yet Patricia pondered his meaning. Had he been referring to her retort or the realization of appreciative, shared laughter?

"We have an entire week to rattle around in," he observed, sipping his fresh cup of coffee. "How would you like to spend it?"

Once again, Patricia was alerted by the watchful expression in his eyes. She knew, instinctively, that he was expecting a rebuff from her. And, once again, she surprised him, pleasantly.

"In self-indulgence." One dark, arched brow nudged her into elaborating. "As I'm sure you do, I live on a pretty tight schedule." His nod was barely perceptible. "I haven't had a real vacation in years, ever since I've been with the company, in fact."

"And?" Peter was obviously still waiting for the ax to drop.

"And I'd like to do whatever takes our fancy at any given moment." Afraid he'd respond by stating the most obvious of his preferences, Patricia held her breath. Fortunately, he replied immediately.

"My first fancy is to clean this mess up, then have a long nap." Peter's smile banished her tension. "I didn't sleep worth a damn last night." His smile grew into a grin. "After we're rested," he continued, making it clear he was fully aware of her own restless night, "we can play it by ear. Does that meet with your approval?"

Relief shimmered through Patricia, releasing the last of the tension, brightening her eyes.

"Yes, that meets with my approval."

It was a beginning. Though neither Patricia nor Peter dared predict the outcome of their week, they were both eager to begin the week in harmony. Smiling in tenuous accord, they rose and started to clear the table.

Six

A soft spring breeze drifted into the room from under the window Patricia had raised two inches before crawling into the bed. It brushed against her cheek with a feather stroke, coaxing her from the depths of slumber. Patricia woke feeling wonderfully refreshed.

A tiny frown marred her brow as she wondered about the time. She was unable to judge by the light coming through the drawn curtains; it could have been early morning or evening.

Patricia discounted morning; it had been morning when she'd finally lost the battle to sleep. Revitalized, she tossed back the covers and sat up on the side of the bed, her gaze darting to the small clock on the bedside table. The tiny hands stood at seven-fifteen.

Seven-fifteen! Good grief! Patricia stared at the clock's face in sheer amazement. It had been somewhere around 7:00 a.m. when she'd murmured good-night to Peter! Had she slept the entire day away? An empty sensation in the pit of her stomach indicated that she probably had.

What must Peter be thinking of her by now? The question sent Patricia rushing into the bathroom, and kept her rushing through her makeup and dressing regimen. She didn't slow down until she walked from the bedroom.

The house had the air of desertion. Moving with her usual brisk stride, Patricia descended the stairs, her senses alert for the sounds of occupancy. There was nothing, not a murmur, until she approached the kitchen. The rustle of paper reached her ears as she reached the archway into the room.

Blinking in surprise, Patricia paused in the archway. Peter was sitting at the table reading the newspaper, his fingers curled around a steaming mug of coffee. But what startled Patricia was his attire, or lack of it. His only covering was the

silky robe he'd worn on their wedding night—
was it only last night? she thought in amazement. His hair was tousled. His face was shadowed by a night's growth of beard. The lapels of
his robe gaped apart, revealing a V of dark chest
curls. A finer sprinkling of hair covered his bare
legs.

As Patricia registered every detail of Peter's
appearance all the moisture in her mouth and
throat evaporated.

Coffee! Juice! Water! She suddenly needed
something to drink. Dragging her gaze from his
blatantly masculine body, Patricia, attempting to
look super cool, made a dash for the coffee
maker.

"Good morning."

Patricia's hand froze in midair an inch from
the handle of the glass pot. Good morning? A
frown of consternation drew her delicate brows
together. Good morning? Her frown deepening,
she turned to face Peter. Surely she hadn't slept
the clock around twice! she thought, uncer-
tainly.

"What time is it?"

"Seven-forty." Peter regarded her expression-
lessly.

Patricia's wide-eyed stare revealed her confusion. "What day is it?" she asked, hesitantly.

"Monday." Peter's lips twitched with amusement.

"Monday!" she exclaimed, her voice squeaky with disbelief. "What happened to Sunday?"

Peter's amusement overflowed into laughter. "Except for breakfast—" he chuckled "—I'm afraid we slept Sunday away."

"We?" Patricia latched onto the one word.

"We," Peter confirmed with a nod. "I woke up twenty minutes ago." His eyes gleamed. "Since you were in the shower, I decided to fix the coffee and catch up on the news."

Digesting the information, Patricia absently poured a cup of coffee for herself before walking to the table. "And what is the news?" she asked as she slid onto a chair.

Peter's smile was dry. "Same old thing. The market's up—as of closing Friday. There's talk about taxes—" his smile turned wry "—again. The basketball play-offs are heating up... etcetera."

Though Patricia returned his smile, hers was more vague than wry. She was simply too distracted to appreciate his droll commentary on the news. "I just can't believe it," she muttered, more to herself than to him.

"That the basketball play-offs are heating up?" Peter inquired politely. "Or the talk about the taxes?"

Patricia shook her head impatiently. "I can't believe that it's Monday morning and I'm sitting here doing nothing."

"Ah—" Peter nodded in understanding. "I know what you mean. It is a strange feeling, not having to hit the floor running in a race against the clock." He grinned crookedly. "I felt odd and disoriented when I got up. Give it a few minutes," he advised. "You'll get used to it."

"But what are we going to do all week?" Patricia didn't hear the plaintive note in her voice.

Peter stared at her a moment before replying. "I distinctly remember you saying we would do whatever takes our fancy." There was a careful note of neutrality woven in his tone that caught her attention. "You've had second thoughts?" he went on, a hint of challenge breaking through.

"No," she denied, "but . . ."

"But?" Peter persisted.

Patricia sighed, then admitted, "I can't honestly say that anything takes my fancy."

Compassion softened Peter's tight lips. Wondering what sort of life-style she maintained that precluded fanciful moments, he gave in to the impulse to slide his palm over her hand. Patricia's startled gaze flew to his eyes.

"You can't think of one thing you've put off doing?" he asked softly.

"No." Patricia shook her head, then looked down at the broad hand covering her own. "Except . . ." her voice trailed away.

"Except?" Peter prompted.

Patricia's lips curved in a deprecating smile. "It's silly." She glanced up, shrugging dismissively.

"All right," he answered, "we'll do something silly. What is it?"

"You won't like it." Patricia couldn't deny the smile that tugged at her lips. "I doubt any man would."

"Try me," he said, returning her tiny smile.

"I want to go shopping."

"Shopping?" Peter stared at her blankly. "What's silly about that?" Before she could respond, he tacked on, "It may be boring, but not silly."

"But you haven't heard where I want to shop," she pointed out, releasing the tight rein she was holding on the smile.

"New York?" Peter frowned when she shook her head slowly. "Paris?" He arched his brows, bringing soft laughter to her lips. But again she shook her head. "Okay," he sighed. "I give up, where do you want to shop?"

"In the factory outlets."

"Factory outlets?" he repeated, confused. "What factory outlets? Where?"

"In Reading." Patricia was laughing openly now. "I told you you wouldn't like it."

"Wait a minute!" Peter held up one hand. "I didn't say I didn't like it." Actually, he detested shopping, anywhere. But, outlets! Peter successfully hid a shudder. "If that's what you want to do, then that's what we'll do."

Less than two hours later Patricia and Peter had left the environs of Philadelphia behind and were driving west on Route 422 toward Reading and the outlet shops.

The first green buds of spring colored the landscape. The breeze wafting in from the partially open car window brushed gently over her cheek. Patricia sighed with a contentment she was unwilling to examine. Here, now, she was content. The very fact that the man beside her was closely related to her feeling of well-being was the reason she was unwilling to examine her odd sense of satisfaction.

They spoke little during the hour-long drive, yet there was no sensation of unease or constraint. Patricia didn't want to examine the absence of strain, either. Nor did she want to recall how very long it had been since she had felt comfortable while in the company of a man—let alone a man who just happened to be her husband!

On entering the city, it became evident to Patricia that Peter was not unfamiliar with the area. He barely glanced at the brightly colored markers, clearly displayed at key intersections, directing motorists to the famous outlet centers where retail manufacturers offered merchandise for sale at greatly reduced prices.

"You've been here before." Though expecting an answer, Patricia made her query more a statement than a question.

"Many times." Peter spared her a glance as he brought the car to a stop at a red light. "I lived here for a few weeks while consulting for a local firm."

"Have you ever shopped in the outlets?" Patricia asked eagerly.

"Well—" Peter's lips took a downward curve "—let's just say I've been in them. I didn't actually shop."

Patricia shifted on the seat to face him, her normally cool eyes warmed to a smoky gray. "Are there really as many bargains to be found in the stores as I've heard?" Her voice was light with anticipation.

Before answering, Peter drove into a parking lot near the center located in the northeast section of the city. Casting a glance at her expectant expression, he pulled on the hand brake, then, reaching a decision, he turned to her. Peter's curiosity had been aroused when Patricia had admitted to her "silly" fancy. Now it got the better of him.

"I knew business was bad at Langdon," he said, "but I hadn't thought it was so bad you were reduced to hunting bargains."

"But—" Patricia exclaimed even as he continued.

"Patricia, I can afford to take you shopping anywhere you wish to go. You do not need to hunt bargains." He said the final word as if it caused a bad taste in his mouth.

Peter had no idea of what kind of reaction his flat statement would bring, but he certainly didn't expect a burst of delighted laughter.

Enjoying his frown of consternation, Patricia brought her mirth under control. "Peter, I know I don't *need* to hunt for bargains. I probably won't even buy anything." She hesitated an instant, then confessed. "I simply love to shop and I use it as a means of escape, especially when I feel pressured."

Peter's frown deepened. "A means of escape? I'm not quite sure I understand what you mean."

Patricia lifted one shoulder in a half shrug. "Some people drink to escape. Others lose themselves in movies, TV or books. I . . . shop."

For some inexplicable reason, Peter felt honored by her disclosure. His unbending, unyielding, very own Lady Ice had admitted to a weakness! Perhaps, just perhaps, Patricia wasn't solid ice to the core. And perhaps, if she hid a tiny ember deep inside, he could eventually fan it into a responsive flame. Peter smiled with the satisfaction his conjecture afforded him. His smile widened as he pushed the car door open.

"Okay, we'll shop." As Patricia stepped onto the macadamized lot, he gestured toward a four-story, red-brick factory building that took up half a city block. "There's your escape. Go to it."

Some six hours and countless stores later, Peter was ruing his expansive invitation. Strolling beside his wife in yet another outlet center, this grouping of buildings on the west side of the city, Peter came to the conclusion that, when Patricia shopped, she didn't fool around. With single-minded purpose that both surprised and amused him, Patricia scrutinized discounted merchandise ranging from filmy undergarments to both soft and molded luggage bearing famous labels. She even bought a few items—luggage, not lingerie.

Fighting back laughter, Peter had assumed a serious expression when she'd exclaimed over the price of a matched set of suitcases. His solemn mien didn't fool her.

"Peter, I looked at a set exactly like this several months ago!" she insisted, examining the luggage for flaws. "And the price on the set was almost double."

Bemused by this unexpected facet of her character, or what he'd perceived as her character, Peter absently reached for his billfold but, before he could withdraw the amount necessary to cover the purchase, Patricia whipped out a credit card to hand to the salesclerk.

As he waited for the transaction to be completed, Peter stood to one side, his expression pensive as he studied his wife. How strange, he mused, sliding an appreciative glance over her impeccably attired, slender body. To the most discerning glance, Patricia appeared ultracool, utterly remote and completely self-assured. Peter had not missed the reaction his wife had elicited from the majority of the people she'd spoken to during the course of the day. Without exception, the reaction to her had been one of grudging respect and reserved friendliness. It seemed as if Patricia's poise intimidated people.

Peter swept another narrow-eyed glance over Patricia's elegant length. Yes, he decided, intimidating described her perfectly. And yet, this very same intimidating woman had just proven herself capable of a near childlike excitability over a shopping expedition. Very strange in—

At that moment, Peter's thoughts were sent scattering by the brilliant smile Patricia gave him as she turned to him, her purchase completed. His breath became lodged somewhere between his chest and his suddenly dry throat. The rest of

his body responded with equal force. His limbs
felt weak, while his masculinity strengthened.

Damn, she's beautiful! Even as the thought
filled his mind, Peter felt a growing sense of
amazement at the intensity of his response to her.

"Peter?"

Requiring more effort than he would have believed possible, Peter pulled himself together.
Straightening away from the display table he'd
been leaning against, he managed a faint smile.

"I'm sorry, I was thinking." He excused his
inattention. "All finished?"

"Yes," Patricia answered, a frown drawing
her brows together. "Are you all right?"

Fully aware he couldn't answer, *Not really,
you see I'm having an uncomfortable libido ex-
plosion,* Peter adopted a bland expression. "You
mean, besides the fact that I may be starving?"
he asked innocently.

Surprising him further by yet another unchar-
acteristic reaction, Patricia's eyes grew wide and
she flushed with embarrassment. "Oh, Peter, I
am sorry! I promised you we'd stop soon for
lunch, didn't I?"

"Mmm," Peter murmured, smiling in spite of
his attempts to contain his amusement. Raising
his arm, he glanced at the gold watch circling his

wrist. "That was at least four hours ago," he taunted. "It is now going on five and my stomach is running on empty."

"It's too late for lunch," Patricia said contritely.

"Right." Collecting two of the cases, Peter started for the store entrance.

"And too early for dinner." After accepting the smallest case from the clerk, Patricia hurried after him.

"Wrong." Holding the door open for her with his shoulder, Peter grinned as she exited the store. Following the enticing sway of her hips as she headed for the car, Peter elaborated on his brief response. "There are actually people who sit down to dinner before seven in the evening. I doubt there's a restaurant in this city that isn't serving dinner at this very minute."

Patricia came to an abrupt halt, nearly causing Peter to plow into her. The gray eyes, which had sparkled with good humor, now glittered with impatience.

"Before we take another step," she said grittily, "let me enlighten you on a few points, Mr. Vanzant. First—" she raised one finger "—I am well aware of the fact that the majority of the populace have their evening meal between five and six o'clock most days." As she paused to draw breath, she held up another finger. "And secondly, regardless of what you may think, I am not, and have never been, a snob." Spinning away from him, she strode to the car.

Startled, and yet amused by her outburst, Peter stood stock-still for an instant before trailing after her. "I didn't accuse you of being a snob," he said, coming up beside her to unlock the car door for her.

Patricia flicked a glance at him. "You didn't have to say it; what you meant came through loud and clear." Lifting her chin, she slid onto the passenger seat.

Releasing a harsh breath, and wondering why he was bothering, Peter stashed the luggage in the trunk then moved to join her in the car. "Patricia, look at me." Shifting around, Peter reached out to grasp her rigidly held chin. His clasp gentle but firm, he drew her averted head around. "Apologies do not come easy for me but, if I've offended you, I'm sorry. Insulting you was not my intention."

Arrested by his compelling gaze, the softness of his deep voice, Patricia sat absolutely still. Unable to break the visual contact, she felt her breath grow shallow. A warmth suffused her skin where his fingers rested, then spread into her cheeks and down her throat to her shoulders. With a growing sense of amazement, Patricia felt her breasts grow taut, the tips begin to tingle. She couldn't speak, not so much as a murmur of protest, as he slowly lowered his head to hers. Peter was going to kiss her—and she was going to let him do it!

His mouth touched hers, lightly, gently. His lips made no demand; his tongue stroked her lower lip but did not challenge the closed portals. He didn't move as much as an inch closer to her.

In actual time the kiss lasted less than a full minute. Inside Patricia, the kiss traveled through years, shaking the foundations of the layers of ice she had so painstakingly built. Patricia imagined she could hear the silent crack of the fault caused by the intense inner warmth. Her imaginings confused, frightened and instilled a sense of relief in her at one and the same time.

Drawing his head back from hers, Peter concentrated on the very ordinary actions of turning to face the wheel, inserting the key into the ignition and starting the engine, thereby avoiding having to examine his extraordinary reactions of tenderness, protectiveness and intense arousal generated by the brief, chaste, closed-lips kiss.

"I will not apologize for the kiss." Peter was mildly shocked by the raw edge on his tone. He was even more shocked by the tremor humming through every muscle and tendon in his body and by the heavy, heated flow of blood through every vein he possessed.

"I haven't asked you to." Patricia's tone was steady, if subdued.

The silence inside the car contrasted starkly with the cacophony of noises from the increasing flow of traffic outside. Captive of their own jumbled thoughts, neither Patricia nor Peter noticed the sounds swirling around them until a loud blast from a car horn shattered the reverie of each.

"Damn fool!" Peter gritted the exclamation through clenched teeth as a motorcyclist darted around and in front of him. Controlling the car expertly, Peter managed to avoid striking the biker, who continued on his way, weaving in and out of the congested traffic.

"Too close," Patricia breathed, shaken by the near miss.

"Yes," Peter hissed in agreement, "and I've had it. I'm hungry, and I sure as hell don't need this agitation. Early or not, we're going to have dinner.''

Fortunately Patricia was also hungry for, after skimming his taut jaw with a sidelong glance, she realized that argument would gain her nothing but trouble.

"Do you know of a restaurant nearby?" she inquired, after allowing him some time to calm down.

"I remember several, but there's a place in particular I'd like you to see." Peter gestured toward the low mountain rising behind the city. "It's perched up there."

From where they were in relation to the city, the only edifice Patricia could see was a pagoda set on top of the mountain. "Are you referring to that building up there?"

Peter smiled and shook his head. "No. That pagoda is a well-known landmark and tourist attraction. It's worth seeing, but we'll leave that for another day." Pulling up at a stop sign, he slanted a teasing look at her. "The restaurant we're going to is set back farther in the hills." At her expression of disappointment, he went on soothingly, "I promise you you'll enjoy it. It's a castle."

"A castle?" she said, skeptically arching one brow.

"Mmm." Peter grinned. "I think you'll like it."

Patricia didn't like the restaurant—she loved it. And it was indeed a castle. Nestled in the wooded hills, the imposing gray stone building might have been in a European country, instead of in a midsize city in Pennsylvania.

"Will this do for an early dinner?" Peter teased as they approached the entrance from the parking area.

"It would do for Henry the Second's Christmas court." Patricia laughed, her bright gaze surveying the turreted structure. "But will they accommodate us without a reservation?"

They not only would, but did . . . with flourish of old-world grace.

The good-looking, soft-spoken maître d' assured them of a table in the library dining room within a matter of minutes. While waiting, Patricia glanced around appreciatively, feeling as if she'd been transported back through the centuries by stepping inside the large reception hall. A smile twitched her lips as she studied a gleaming suit of armor standing sentinel near a staircase. Flicking down, her amused gaze skimmed over the very twentieth-century, lightweight pantsuit she'd chosen to wear that morning. Lifting her gaze, she perused the casual slacks, silk shirt and sport jacket Peter was wearing. In this setting, she and Peter appeared out of sync!

"Patricia?" Peter's low voice was laced with amusement.

"Yes?" Patricia blinked and found herself gazing into sparkling dark eyes that would have beguiled in any period of time.

"Our table is ready." He indicated the patiently waiting maître d' with a slight nod of his head.

"There is no reason to hurry here," the elegantly attired man murmured, his hooded eyes complimenting Patricia's cool blond beauty. "Please feel free to enjoy the castle and, if you have time, seek me out after dinner. I'd be happy to escort you to the dungeon."

"The dungeon!" Patricia exclaimed over a burst of startled laughter. "You have a real dungeon here?" Thoroughly captivated, she moved to walk beside the man, questioning him as he ushered them past several interesting-looking rooms of varying sizes. Since Peter was left little choice but to trail after them, she was unaware of the annoyance tightening his features.

"And of course," the maître d' elaborated on the dungeon, "it has iron implements of fiendish design." The room he led them to was large, boasting a wide fireplace and walls lined with books. "Naturally, there is also a ballroom." With a courtly air, he held a chair for her. "Is a castle a castle without a ballroom?"

Murmuring thank you, Patricia seated herself gracefully, then glanced up to smile at the hovering man. "I don't know," she admitted, "I've never been in a castle before."

Patricia discovered his eyes were sky-blue when he ran a warmly caressive gaze over her. "Then we are honored that you chose this one to make your debut in." Bowing slightly, he flicked a glance at Peter, then murmured, "Your waiter will be with you presently, sir." His eyes warmed again as he shifted his attention back to Patricia. "Enjoy your dinner."

"Fawning jerk." Peter's dismissive growl drew Patricia's startled eyes to his scowling face.

"Peter!" she protested. "He was very nice!"

"Nice?" Peter sneered. "He was practically eating you alive with his eyes."

"Really?" Patricia's smile was innocently seductive. "How interesting."

"You're a married woman." Peter's tone was deadly. "You are *my* wife, Patricia. Remember it."

Taking exception to his tone, Patricia turned on the ice. "That sounds very much like an order," she said in a chilling tone. "And I don't take orders from any man, Peter. I suggest you remember that."

Suddenly the castle, the entire day lost its charm for her. Blaming him, Patricia withdrew into her safe, cold shell. Attack came naturally—he was a man, wasn't he?

"Furthermore, might I remind you, I am your wife in name only. Remember *that*, Mr. Vanzant."

The change in Peter was as abrupt and chilling as it had been in her. Before her eyes, the pleasant, easygoing companion she had spent the day with was replaced by a forbidding, arrogant man.

Their gazes clashed then held, glacial gray warring with glittering dark brown. Patricia felt coolly assured of maintaining the visual battle until Peter said the one thing capable of undermining her confidence.

"Since I have no intention of permitting my wife to openly flirt with other men, I think it's time I consummated this inconvenient marriage."

Visibly shocked and secretly shaken by his statement, Patricia hastily glanced around to check if any of the patrons had overheard. Assured by their obvious disinterest that they hadn't, she brought her icy gaze back to him.

"Think again," she snapped softly. "If—and when—this marriage is *ever* consummated, I will decide the time and the place."

The appearance of their waiter prevented the response Peter was about to make. His set expression sending little warning shivers racing down her spine, Patricia sighed with relief and thanked providence for the arrival of the waiter.

Considering the charm and ambience of the castle, the meal should have been most enjoyable, but, with the thick tension shimmering between Patricia and Peter, it was barely tolerable. The food, though expertly prepared, was barely tasted. The tall, impressive couple who exited the restaurant were barely recognizable as the smiling duo who had entered ninety minutes earlier. Needless to say, they did not inspect the ballroom or the dungeon—even though Patricia felt certain Peter would be happy to pitch her into the latter and forget he'd ever met her.

A wall of constraint barred conversation between them as they drove to Peter's suburban Philadelphia town house. The silence prevailed as they carried the newly purchased luggage into the narrow foyer.

"Leave them here," Peter directed tersely, stashing the cases along the white-wainscoted wall. "I'll put them away tomorrow."

"As you wish." Tight with tension, Patricia still managed a careless-looking shrug as she walked to the open-backed staircase. "I'm tired. I'm going to my room." She arched one pale brow mockingly. "If you will excuse me?" Her tone said clearly that she didn't give a damn either way. "Good night, Mr. Vanzant. I'll see you in the morning."

Think again. Peter silently repeated her earlier retort.

Seven

Determination settled in Peter as he watched the fluid motion of Patricia's body as she ascended the stairs, her slim fingers trailing along the polished wood banister. As if he could feel the light touch of her fingertips, Peter shivered with a tingle that skipped the length of his spine. The tingle grew, radiating out to encompass his entire body. Peter sighed with relief when Patricia turned at the landing to disappear from sight as she went to her room.

Breathing raggedly, he drew his gaze from the empty staircase. Suddenly parched, he strode

into the large high-ceilinged living room. As a
rule, the tranquil beauty of the room, decorated
in earth tones and furnished with man-size chairs
and an extra-long sofa, had a soothing effect on
Peter. This evening, he didn't notice the warmth
of color or decor. His gaze fastened on the hand-
carved credenza, Peter made for it and reached
for a decanter of Scotch. He pulled the cut-glass
stopper then, with a decisive shake of his head,
replaced it again. Pivoting away from the cabinet, he strode through the open dining area and
into the kitchen.

"You want to keep a clear head, Vanzant," he
muttered, crossing to the refrigerator. Yanking
open the door, he withdrew a half-full quart of
milk. Drinking directly from the carton, he
emptied it in a few deep swallows. The cool liquid eased the tightness in Peter's throat.

Now, he thought grimly, retracing his steps
back to the staircase in the foyer, *I think it's time
to ease the tightness in my body.*

Peter heard the splash of water as he walked by
the bathroom. His lips compressing, he paused
to consider his options.

Should he join her in the bath? The idea was
appealing and exciting. Peter had shed his jacket
and was fumbling with the buttons on his shirt

before he reached his bedroom a few yards down the hallway. Flinging his clothes onto a chair, he'd stripped down to his brief shorts before giving thought to another option open to him.

Perhaps his chances would be better for successful seduction if he waited until she was finished bathing, relaxed and hopefully reclining on the bed.

This second option had even more appeal. It was definitely more exciting. Picturing Patricia as she'd looked on their wedding night, glowing from her bath, slim and sexy in a sheer nightgown and peignoir, Peter opted to wait.

Deciding he could do with a shower, Peter slid his thumbs under the elastic band hugging his hips and slid the briefs over his tight buttocks and down his muscular flanks. Stepping out of the briefs, he ran a hand up his thickly haired chest, rubbed absently then continued on up his throat to test the stubble on his jaw.

He could do with a shave as well, he mused. Scooping up the robe laying at the foot of the bed, he strolled into the hall and to the other bathroom near the top of the stairs. Moments later, anticipation humming through his system, Peter stepped under an invigoratingly cool shower. And still later, as he carefully shaved his cheeks and jaw clean of all roughness, he made himself a solemn promise: tonight he would take unto himself a wife—whether said wife wanted a husband or not!

Patricia was thirsty but, since she was also wary of another encounter with Peter, she decided to forgo the glass of white wine she was longing for and slake her thirst with a glass of water from the bathroom tap.

Naked, she walked into her room in search of the scented lotion she smoothed on her body after bathing. Massaging the cool lotion into the skin on her shoulders, Patricia shivered as a vision formed of Peter's angry expression when she'd bid him a chill good-night. A delicate tremor rippled from her nape to the base of her spine. Peter's frustration had been like a palpable force washing over her. Smoothing lotion onto her arms, she fought an urge to run from him and the danger he represented.

Poised with one foot propped on the edge of the bed, she stroked the emollient into her leg absently as her mind replayed images of the day and the man she'd spent it with. Warmth suffused her body as Patricia remembered the sweetness of his kiss.

The barely perceptible sound of the connecting door opening froze Patricia's hand in its upward stroke on her leg. A shiver of premonition feathered her shoulders an instant before she heard Peter's sharply indrawn breath.

For a long moment she went absolutely blank then, her leg and arm moving simultaneously, she slid her foot from the bed and reached for her nightgown. Shielding her nakedness with the next-to-useless sheer material, she glared at him from eyes chilled with challenge.

"What do you want?" Patricia immediately regretted the question, simply because the answer was obvious. Everything about him fairly shouted his intent.

"I want my rights as your husband." Though soft, Peter's tone was steely with determination.

Patricia didn't flinch or even blink. Standing tall and proud, she smothered the protest that filled her mind and attempted reason as a means of escaping the inevitable. "I told you I needed time." Clutching the filmy gown to her chest, Patricia despaired of her tremulous tone.

"And now I'm telling you that your time has run out," he countered, moving into the room.

A feeling of fatalism washing over her, Patricia forced herself to remain still as Peter slowly walked to her. The muscles in her stomach clenched when he tossed the silky robe from his body.

Fully clothed, Peter Vanzant was an imposing man. Naked and aroused, he was all magnificent male—more male than Patricia felt capable of dealing with.

"Peter..." Her breath broke on a gasp as he reached out to gently pry her fingers from the nightgown.

"Patricia..." He mimicked her breathless tone as he tossed the sheer garment aside.

Swallowing roughly, Patricia wet her dry lips with a flick of her tongue. His searing gaze followed her action, drying the moisture even as she slicked it onto her lips.

"I want to feel your tongue on my lips." His tone was rough with passion. His eyes glittered with need. Raising his hand, Peter outlined her lips with his index finger. Watching her, feeling the moistness of her breath on his hand, his eyes darkened to dense black, revealing his heightened desire. "I want to feel your tongue in my mouth."

"Peter, I can't—I won't!" As she gasped the refusal, Patricia felt her pulse hammering, experienced a sensation of heat rushing through her veins.

"You can," Peter corrected, his finger leaving a trail of fire as it slid from her lips to her breasts, "and you will."

Though Patricia shook her head in mute denial, a shudder traveled through her body when his fingers captured the tip of one breast. Her breathing came in short puffs as he slowly lowered his head to hers, brushing his lips over hers once, twice, then once more.

"Damn it, Patricia," he groaned harshly, nipping her lip gently, "open your mouth for me!" He fused his lips to hers when she automatically complied.

Patricia had been kissed deeply before—long years before—but never had she experienced this sudden weakness in her limbs, or the loud rushing sound in her ears, reverberating with Peter's order muttered into her mouth.

"Do it now, wife. I want to feel your tongue inside my mouth."

With the play of teasing, tormenting fingers luring her on, Patricia hesitantly slipped the tip of her tongue over the smoothness of his bottom lip and the roughness of his teeth.

"Deeper," Peter moaned, wrapping his free arm around her waist to draw her body into full contact with his own. "I want to feel and taste all of it."

Patricia hovered on the edge of uncertainty for an instant, then she pulled away from him abruptly.

"No!" Shaking her head to underline the sharp denial, she skirted around him and fled to the other side of the room.

"Patricia, what the hell ...!" Peter raked his fingers through his damp hair, ruffling the neatly brushed swath of gleaming black.

Breathing deeply, unmindful of her pale nakedness, Patricia watched him warily. "Did you actually believe I wouldn't know what you were asking?" she demanded, her voice tight with emotion.

"I haven't the vaguest idea what you're talking about!" Peter came perilously close to shouting. Also unconcerned with his lack of covering, he faced her squarely, hands on his hips. "One minute you're warm and willing," he accused, "and the next minute you're frozen again. What are you trying to do to me?"

"*I'm* not trying to do a damn thing!" Patricia denied hotly. "*You* came in here uninvited!"

"But you're my wife!" Now Peter was definitely shouting, and he was flushed with anger. "Whether you'll admit it or not, for a moment there, you *wanted* me to make love to you." His drilling stare challenged her to deny his statement.

Patricia longed to fling a sneering retort at him, but in all honesty she could not. She had felt the sensuous weakness in her limbs, the heat searing her blood, the melting moisture at the heart of her femininity. She *had* wanted him! And the want had been growing ever since he'd kissed her so sweetly in the car that afternoon. But what Peter had offered a moment ago had not been sweetly shared pleasure but domination. Patricia was having none of that! Her stare was stony.

"You did want it," he persisted when she remained silent. "Didn't you?"

"Yes!" Cornered by the truth, Patricia raised her chin regally and faced him defiantly.

Peter frowned in confusion. "Then why the hell did you pull away?" He took a step toward her, then paused when she took one step back. "Patricia." He sighed her name. "Why? What happened to cause that sudden change from warm willingness to icy rejection?"

"You," she said succinctly. "You caused the rejection." Peter's eyes flicked in surprise and she went on relentlessly. "You didn't want mere willingness, Peter. You wanted submission. You were demanding my unconditional surrender." His eyes flickered again, this time with uncertainty. Her voice remote, Patricia stated her position. "I'm as normal as any woman, Peter, and I'm as vulnerable, too. But I will not be owned, not by any man."

"Not even by your husband?"

"Most especially not by my husband."

Since he was expecting it, Peter was not surprised by her emphatic response. He was mildly surprised by the conflicting emotions he was experiencing. Under the circumstances, the conversation was ludicrous. They were both stark naked! Yet, oddly, the absence of clothes seemed to strip away the self-applied veneer of evasion.

Like combatants on either side of a parallel line, Peter and Patricia faced each other—and themselves. Peter was the first one to make a move. His broad chest heaving with a sharply drawn breath, he walked to the edge of the bed and sat down. A wave of his hand indicated the lounge chair to Patricia's right.

"Sit down, Patricia," he invited. "I think it's time for an in-depth discussion."

As if becoming aware of her nakedness at that instant, Patricia stiffened with embarrassment. "I—I'd like to dress." She turned to walk to the closet. Peter's voice halted her in mid-step.

"No!" He met her startled gaze with rock-hard steadiness. "No barriers of any kind, Patricia." His smile was wry. "And, if we dress, we'll assume the barriers with the clothing."

"Peter—" she began, impatience replacing embarrassment.

"Sit down, Patricia." Peter's tone was steely with command. "Please." He felt as if he'd won a minor skirmish when she obeyed after a hesitant pause.

Though Patricia appeared unsure of what to do with her hands, Peter was too busy marshaling his thoughts to suffer the same problem, or even notice that she was having one.

"I've been thinking over what you said," he began slowly. "And I'm afraid your accusation was correct. I *did* want your submission." He frowned, then went on in a low tone, as if talking to himself. "I wanted your surrender from the moment you responded to that maître d'."

"The maître d'!" Astonished, Patricia blinked at him. "I most certainly did not *respond* to him! Not in the way you're implying. I was merely being friendly."

"Yes, I realize that." Peter smiled in self-derision. "I also realize that *he* was merely responding to you in the way any male responds to a beautiful woman."

"Exactly."

Her disgusted tone set off an alarm in Peter's mind. It was the tone she usually acquired when speaking about men. "You don't like men much, do you?" he asked neutrally.

Patricia hesitated, then decided that if he wanted the barriers down, that was precisely what he'd get. "No," she said with blunt honesty. "I don't particularly like men." A mocking smile twisted her lips. "But then, you don't particularly like women, either, do you?"

Peter's amazement was obvious. "Quite the contrary," he swiftly contradicted her. "I like women very much."

"For certain purposes," Patricia sneered.

"Among other things," Peter admitted. "But, as to those certain things, there is nothing wrong with enjoying a mutually satisfying physical relationship."

"With any number of partners?" she shot
back at him.

"There's safety in numbers," he retaliated,
positive she was referring to his reputation. "Just
as you insist no man will ever own you, I have
promised myself that no woman will ever put a
ring through my nose."

On the point of returning his fire, Patricia
paused, her attention caught by something in his
tone. There was an undertone here that she
couldn't put her finger on, a hint of pain she
couldn't quite comprehend. Had some woman
hurt Peter long ago? Hurt him in the same manner in which she herself had been hurt? The possibility was intriguing. But, she mused, would
Peter be willing to admit to the injury if he had
suffered one? Her nakedness completely forgotten, Patricia studied her husband consideringly.

"You have a decidedly crafty look about you."
Peter's eyes narrowed in the way she was quickly
growing accustomed to. "I can't help but wonder what's going on in that gorgeous head of
yours."

Patricia didn't even try to deny the pleasure his
compliment gave her. But she didn't dwell on it
either. She had more important things on her
mind.

"Feeling as you do, why did you agree to my mother's proposition?" Fully expecting him to tell her that he wanted a share of her grandfather's company, Patricia was startled by his candid response.

"*You* were the deciding factor." A small smile relieved the tension on his face. "I certainly didn't need the company. And, in truth, I had no intention of giving Margaret's offer any serious consideration . . . until I walked into your office." His smile changed to a twist of self-mockery. "Everything about you challenged me. I decided on the spot that I would own you." One dark eyebrow inched to a peak. "Feeling as you do about men—" he threw her question back at her "—why did you agree to go along with your mother's proposition?"

"Unlike you, I *did* and do want the company." Patricia paused, then went on in a far less certain tone. "But now, I can't help but wonder, if, subconsciously, I wanted to find out if it was possible to put a ring through the nose of the reputed lady-killer."

Silence as dense as the night blanketed the room for an untold number of minutes. Peter shattered it with a soft, beguiling suggestion.

"Let's make mutually satisfying love, Patricia."

Staring at her hands clasped on her thighs, Patricia jerked her head up to stare at him. "Wh—what?" She could barely speak for the excitement storming her body, tightening her throat.

"I said," he repeated, patting the mattress beside him, "let's make love. Come over here to me. We *are* married. It is going to happen sometime, and we both know it. I want to make love with you. You want to make love with me." His smile coaxed. All the arrogance disappeared, leaving a man. A very attractive man. "We are both vulnerable, in one way or another. Without thoughts or threats of ownership or nose rings, we can begin learning about each other in the most basic way possible for a man and a woman. I promise to never deliberately hurt you, either physically or emotionally." Lifting his hand from the bed, he held it out to her, palm up. "Will you make a beginning with me, Patricia?"

Patricia couldn't resist his entreaty. Peter's offer was infinitely more appealing than yet another long night spent alone in an empty bed.

Not at all sure she was doing the right thing, she rose and slowly walked to the bed—and him.

As she approached him, Peter stretched his length on the bed and opened his arms invitingly. "Come lie with me," he paraphrased in a voice low with gathering passion, "and be my wife."

Bemused and somewhat stunned by the melting process occurring deep within her body, Patricia knelt on the mattress beside him. Feeling weighted, her arms hung limply by her sides. Although she was fully conscious of appearing to offer her body to him, she could not move for, in truth, she had not yet decided to give herself to him.

"Patricia." Peter whispered her name on a softly expelled breath then, clasping her face, he drew her mouth down to his.

This time Peter made no demand of her, either by word or act. Gently, tenderly he molded his lips to hers, taking only what she offered. And, set on fire by the heat of his mouth, Patricia then offered everything.

As if awed by the magnitude of her gift, Peter accepted the prize of her body with hands that trembled as they stroked the silkiness of her skin and with words that praised the perfection of her person.

"Your mouth is sweet," he murmured against her lips, "so very sweet."

In return for his accolade, Patricia parted her lips to give entrance to his searching, hungry tongue.

"Your breasts are exquisitely formed," he whispered, lightly stroking from the outer curve to the swiftly hardening crest. "Your skin has the texture of warm satin."

In reaction to his adoring tone and teasing play, Patricia arched her back to give him free access.

"So slender, so delicate," he praised hoarsely, gliding his palms down her rib cage to her waist. "Yet so deliciously rounded," he continued, cupping her hips firmly.

"Peter—" Patricia breathed his name as his palms warmed the smooth outer line of her thighs. She was shivering, reacting to flames of sensation that seemed to lick through her entire system until she was experiencing a depth of arousal she'd never dreamed her body was capable of.

"What is it, sweet wife?" Peter's low voice was seduction itself. Patricia's shiver gained strength. "What can I give you?" As he murmured the question, his hand skimmed the pearl-toned flesh of her inner thigh. A soft moan was torn from her throat when his stroking fingers found her source of heat.

"Peter..." His name was again wrenched from her, entangled within a deeper moan.

Driven beyond endurance by the expertise of his caressing fingers, Patricia reciprocated impulsively. Lifting her hands, she tentatively, then boldly stroked the warm skin on his long body. As her hands smoothed the taut muscles lacing his flat belly, Peter groaned and arched his hips, silently inviting a more intimate caress.

Patricia hesitated for an instant, then his probing fingers decided the silent issue. Responding to his deepening caress, she took him gently into her palms and stroked his length with a feather-light touch.

"What can I give you?" he repeated with growing urgency, raising his hips in time with her rhythmic stroke.

This time Patricia didn't hesitate at all. Releasing him, she slid her hands up his body as she slowly lowered her own to lie beside him. "Make me your wife, Peter," she pleaded. Clasping his face between her palms, she covered his mouth with her parted lips.

Peter's response was immediate and electrifying. His devouring mouth made a demand Patricia was now more than willing to obey. Loosening her hold on his face, she slid her hands to his shoulders to guide him as he covered her body with his.

"I can't promise you gentleness," he whispered into the honeyed sweetness of her mouth. "I'm too far gone for subtlety." His hair-rough legs caused an exciting tingle on her tender skin as he eased between her thighs. The proof of his confession pressed impetuously against the portal of her femininity, seeking entrance to the heart of her fire.

Aroused to abandonment for the first time in her life, Patricia enticed the passion in him by sinking her fingers into his muscle-corded shoulders and embracing him with her legs.

"Then give me wildness," she invited in a breathless murmur. "Make me wild, too."

It had been nearly ten years since Patricia's body had known the fullness of a man. A softly gasped "Oh" burst from her throat as Peter, acting on her instructions, thrust his body into hers. At her outcry he became still and tense.

"Have I hurt you?" he asked anxiously, concern widening his eyes and tightening the muscles along his jawline.

"No," Patricia hastened to assure him, melting around him as her body grew accustomed to the size and fullness of his. To reinforce her denial, she slid her hands down his back and over his tight buttocks, drawing him into an even deeper embrace. An enticing smile tilted the corners of her lips as she felt him quickening inside her.

"Siren." As if unable to resist her lure, Peter brought his mouth to hers. "I've married a siren," he said in a wondering whisper, moving his body in a ritualistic cadence as old as time. The wonder filling his mind erupted in a joyous laugh. His cool breath filled her mouth. "And she doesn't even realize that she is a siren!"

"What does a siren do, Peter?" Patricia's voice reflected his laughter, her body arched to his cadence.

"Lures men to the ecstasy of death," he responded between ragged breaths, increasing the tempo of his body. "Exactly as you're doing now!" Drawing his head back, Peter gazed at her from eyes dark with mounting passion. "But please don't stop!"

His voice was so low that Patricia could barely hear him. But it didn't matter; she heard the message being sent directly into her body. At one with him, she mirrored his every move, thrilling to the tension, tightening, inside, outside, longing for, yet dreading, the release that would end this most incredible experience she'd ever known.

When the end came it was indeed wild—wild and shattering and freeing. For an endless instant, Patricia was convinced of her ability to fly. Giving herself completely to the joy of the moment, and to Peter, she soared blissfully away from the boundaries of earth and time. Head thrown back, she cried aloud with the first genuine completion she'd ever felt, and smiled in satisfaction as Peter's cry echoed her own.

Returning to reality was not a letdown, but the continuation of pleasure. As her breathing caught up to her heartbeat, Patricia became aware of the pleasing weight of Peter's body resting on hers, of his head pillowed on her breasts, of the soothing sensation of his hand lightly stroking her body from her shoulder to her thigh and of the gentle tug of his lips on the crest of one breast.

Sharing the warmth of afterglow, Patricia smoothed one palm over his wide shoulders, then trailed her fingers the length of his spine, smiling tenderly when he shivered in response.

"You'll start it all over again," he muttered warningly, moistening her quivering flesh with his breath.

"Is that possible—so soon?" Even as she asked, she felt him stir to life inside her. "Peter!" she exclaimed on a tiny yelp of laughter, but moving her body sensuously.

"I wouldn't have thought it possible—so soon," he said, teasing her with a gentle thrust. "But, as should be more than apparent, it would appear it is."

His body was no longer languid but hard and tight with renewed vigor. Raising his chest from hers, he propped the weight of his torso on his forearms. Then, his eyes growing dark with revived passion, he lowered his head. Closing his lips around one aching nipple, he suckled at her breast with greedy hunger.

Peter's intimate touch created a spiraling sensation inside Patricia that spread in ever-widening circles. Reveling in his ministrations, she again abandoned herself to the realm of touch and taste and the sheer joy of sensuality.

Eight

Patricia was sound asleep, her slightly parted lips curved into a tiny satisfied smile. Her warm breath ruffled the wiry swirls of hair and misted the skin on Peter's chest.

Though his body felt pleasantly drained, Peter was wide awake. The fingers of his left hand absently toyed with the tousled blond waves at her temple. His right arm had gone numb over an hour ago.

Peter wished fervently that it had been his mind that had gone numb. But he was alert—

painfully alert. His conscience was reading him
the riot act.

*Okay, master lover, now you've had more of
her than you'd ever hoped she'd allow you to
have. Isn't it time to back away?* His conscience
gibed.

Even with the numbness, Peter managed to
tighten his arm around his sleeping wife in a silent response to the inner query.

No? What courage! conscience sneered. *Aren't
you afraid of having your emotions engaged
along with your active libido?*

Turning his head, Peter gazed at Patricia's
softly relaxed features a moment then closed his
eyes, not to obliterate the taunting voice, but to
hear it more clearly.

*This blond goddess you now call wife is a per-
fection of sculpted ice. You know that, don't
you?* His conscience jabbed relentlessly.

Yes. A spasm of pain flickered across Peter's
face as he made the soundless admission.

Yes. His conscience repeated the one word in
a satisfied purr. *She holds the singular power to
frost you. Do you realize that as well?*

Yes. Peter's breathing grew constrained at the
magnitude of his confession.

Interesting. The purrlike quality of the voice of conscience deepened. *Are you deliberately seeking much-deserved retribution by lying in the embrace of this lady made of ice?*

No! Though silent, Peter's denial came hot and swift.

Then why bother with her? The voice of conscience retorted just as swiftly. *She can do to you what you have done to many of her sex. She can reject you with cold disdain.*

I know. Even without substance, Peter's reply rang tiredly in his mind.

Then why bother with her? Working overtime, conscience persisted. *Why not walk away, as you have so often in the past?*

I can't. Peter knowingly hedged.

Why not? conscience demanded.

I want her more now than before she gave herself to me, Peter admitted mutely. *Damn it! I want her for myself, exclusively. I want to own her!*

Ah. The voice of conscience sighed with relief. *Perhaps there is hope for you after all.*

Patricia woke at dawn. For long moments she lay luxuriating in the warmth of being held spoon fashion against Peter's chest. Discomfort came with mental alertness. Her mind uneasy, she carefully shifted away from him. Though he grumbled and sprawled onto his back, Peter didn't wake up.

Separated by several inches from him, Patricia eased off the edge of the bed. The cool morning air swirled around her nude body, chilling her skin. Staring at her sleeping husband, Patricia silently slipped into his silk robe. As the large robe enveloped her body, the scent of him enveloped her senses, evoking the feel of him, the taste of him. Heat flared inside, making her feel weak with need for him.

Her breathing growing shallow, Patricia stared at the man she had surrendered to and experienced a longing to repeat the performance. She wanted him. It was as simple as that. The difficult part was facing her loss of control.

She could very easily fall in love with this man.

Patricia's body jerked in reaction to the realization. She didn't want to love Peter. She didn't want to love any man. But she was his wife. She had given herself to him with an abandon she hadn't realized she was capable of. And she had gloried in every second of it.

Was it possible? Patricia asked herself. *Could they possibly make the marriage work? Did she want to?*

Staring at the relaxed face of the man who was now her lover as well as her husband, Patricia acknowledged the hollow sensation inside for what it was—an emptiness in her life that needed to be filled. The truth shattered her defenses.

Did she want the marriage to work? Patricia closed her eyes and sighed as the answer whispered in her mind. *Yes.*

Seconds after waking to a room full of spring sunshine and an empty space beside him on the bed, Peter recalled his battle with his conscience.

I want to own her. Groaning aloud, Peter rolled onto his stomach and buried his face in the pillow, which still bore the scent of Patricia's perfume. Closing his eyes, he inhaled her scent.

I want her for myself, exclusively. Peter burrowed more deeply into the pillow to retain the illusion of her presence. Patricia's voice echoed in his mind. "I will not be owned."

By her own admission, Patricia didn't particularly like men. And by her attitude she trusted men even less than she liked them.

But why?

Savoring the combined scents of expensive perfume and exciting woman, Peter flipped onto his back to stare at the stark white ceiling through narrowed eyes.

Patricia was not cold by nature. She had proved that last night. So, if she wasn't cold by nature, that left one conclusion for Peter to reach. His wife, his own lady of ice, was a fraud—a fraud with a meticulously acquired frost.

But why? A frown drew Peter's black brows together over his narrowed eyes. Why was Patricia, the real Patricia, hiding inside a hard casing of ice?

Without considering the fact that he was genuinely interested and concerned for reasons other than physical motivation, Peter flung the tangled covers from his body and sprang from the bed. He had work to do. And his first priority was to find a chisel delicate enough to chip at ice.

Patricia was sitting at the kitchen table, trying to assimilate the printed words in the business section of the morning paper, when Peter ambled into the room.

As it had when she'd slipped into his robe at dawn, his scent teased her senses and played havoc with her reasoning process. But one thought escaped the confusion and sent despair through her. *How did one go about creating a viable marriage?* The blatant fact was, in the interaction of male and female, she was sadly lacking in experience.

Watching him covertly while pretending an interest in the paper, Patricia was astounded by the conflicting emotions storming her defenses. He was, unquestionably, very good to look at. He was, also unquestionably, very good in bed. The fire responsively flaring to life in her body testified to Peter's expertise in the art of love-making.

"Are you in there?" Peter's tone teased. The tip of one finger tapped against the newspaper, rattling it—and her.

"Yes." Lowering the shield, Patricia gazed at him solemnly. "Good morning."

"Is it, Patricia?" he asked seriously. "After last night, is it a good morning?" The teasing note was gone, replaced by an anxious under-tone.

Patricia stared at him pensively, pondering hidden meanings in his seemingly forthright question. Was Peter merely asking the obvious, his ego needing to confirm that she was satisfied? No. Patricia rejected the idea even as it formed. Peter was far too perceptive to have misjudged her contentment after the fact.

Patricia controlled the urge to squirm on the padded kitchen chair. Was he perhaps wondering if her attitude toward men in general and him in particular had softened after being exposed to his fire? she mused, maintaining his steady regard. Probably. Patricia viewed her second theory more favorably.

If her assumptions were accurate, then was he holding out for the unconditional surrender he had demanded from her earlier in the evening? Most likely. Patricia followed her theory to its logical conclusion. Peter wanted the morning to be every bit as good for her as the night had been. But did Peter want a wife this morning or a conquest?

"Damn it, Pat! Answer me!" The use of the nickname, more than his impatient tone, shattered her reverie. "Is it a good morning for you?"

"Yes, Peter." Patricia smiled, allowing him a tantalizing hint of both wife and conquest, while concealing the whole of either one. "It's a lovely morning, warm with the promise of spring. And it's your turn to indulge your fancy." As she spoke the invitation, Patricia prayed he would not disappoint her with the obvious response.

Her prayer was heard—either by a higher being or an astute husband.

"My immediate fancy is for breakfast. I'm starving." A silent sigh of relief compressed Peter's chest as he turned away to walk to the fridge. He had guessed Patricia had feared his answer would be blatantly sexual. By her softened expression, he had guessed correctly.

You're learning, Vanzant. Smiling to himself, Peter removed a carton of eggs from the fridge. As he reached for the bacon he added, cautioningly, *Now don't screw up!*

"Scrambled or fried?" he asked, grinning as he wiggled the egg carton.

"Fried." Patricia grinned back. "I'm a closet egg dipper."

Peter felt the force of her impish grin all the way down to his socks. "Oh, well, in that case, I'm afraid I can't let this chance go by to blackmail you into helping me prepare breakfast." His dark eyes gleamed with good humor and sheer devilry.

"Blackmail me?" Patricia frowned but got up to help. "How could you blackmail me?" Walking over to the cabinet, she managed to retrieve a frying pan and toss a questioning look at him at the same time.

"I'll tell everyone you know that you're a secret egg dipper," he taunted, plopping butter into the pan. "Imagine their reactions!" He assumed an expression of shocked astonishment. "I mean, the very cool, very correct Patricia Lycaster Vanzant, a closet egg dipper!" He widened his eyes, then fluttered his thick, blunt eyelashes at her.

Patricia fought her mirth for a moment, then it burst from her in musical laughter. For an instant, mesmerized by the lilting sound, Peter stared at her, an ache of wanting to belong, to be included in every aspect of her life, unfurling inside him. Then, grasping the moment of friendly communion, he laughed with her.

"And what do you suppose the reaction would be—" Patricia returned his banter as the laughter faded "—if I told everyone you know that you can tease and clown just like normal men?"

Peter contrived to look offended. "I'm abnormal?"

Patricia broke four eggs into the sizzling pan before replying. "From the information I've gathered, I'd say you were light-years ahead of the normal man."

Turning the bacon curling on the grill between the burners, Peter eyed her warily, uncertain whether to feel insulted or complimented. The bacon neatly turned, he homed in on what he considered the salient point of her statement.

"You gathered information about me?"

Cursing her imprudence, Patricia shied away from his drilling stare. "Of course," she muttered, poking the edges of the bubbling eggs.

"And what did you learn?" Interest, not anger, was revealed by his tone.

"Well..." Stalling for time to compose her thoughts, Patricia transferred the eggs to two plates. "I learned that you earned your reputation as the best consultant in the business by applying sharp intelligence with sheer hard work." She held the plates while he drained excess fat from the bacon onto folded paper towels.

"And?" Peter prompted, dividing the bacon equally onto the plates.

"I learned you earned your reputation with women in exactly the same way." Turning away from him, she headed for the table. "Can you get the toast?"

"Yeah, sure," he murmured, obviously distracted. When he joined her at the table he had the toast and the coffeepot. "I'd appreciate clarification of your last remark, please," he said, filling her cup with the steaming brew.

Patricia busied her hands by buttering the toast. "Your breakfast will get cold," she pointed out, employing delaying tactics.

"I have no difficulty listening while I eat," he countered.

Asking herself why she was even bothering to spare his feelings, Patricia gave up the effort. "The information I garnered was that you applied every bit as much intelligence and hard work to learning the art of lovemaking as you did to the business of consultancy." She grew warm and uncomfortable, but she continued. "I was told that you speak the words of lovemaking beautifully, while never speaking the words of love."

Peter was quiet for so long Patricia finally glanced up from the crisp bacon she was crumbling onto her plate. From the heat in her face, she knew her cheeks were pink, which surprised her. Patricia rarely blushed. But what surprised her even more was the red stain crawling up Peter's taut cheeks.

"I have no defense against what you were told." Peter met her questioning stare directly. And, despite his assurance, his breakfast lay congealing on the plate. Before continuing, he poked at the eggs with his fork. "I have never told a woman that I was in love with her...simply because I didn't love any one of them.'' Emotions flickered across his face. ''I came close once, but...'' His voice trailed away and he smiled in a sad way that touched a soft spot in Patricia.

''I'm sorry, Peter,'' she said contritely. ''I—you owe me no explanations.''

''I know.'' Slicing the edge of his fork through the end of an egg, he speared it and brought it to his mouth. As he chewed the food, his lips twisted with distaste. ''It's cold,'' he said, pushing the plate away.

''I'm sorry,'' Patricia repeated, gazing at him helplessly.

''I'm not.'' There was strength in his tone and steel in his dark eyes that had nothing to do with the cold breakfast. Noting her confusion, Peter went on, ''I'm not sorry for the way I've lived my life,'' he clarified. ''The information you gathered was correct. There have been a lot of women in my life. I regret only one of them.''

Suddenly it didn't matter that their breakfast had gone cold. Patricia wasn't hungry anymore. There was an uncomfortable ache uncoiling in her stomach. An ache for Peter. An ache for the unknown woman Peter regretted hurting. An ache for herself.

"If you're finished, I'll clear this mess away." Pushing her chair back with unnecessary force, Patricia stood and began collecting dishes. Her stride brisk, she moved to the sink. Her actions unnaturally awkward, she scraped the barely touched food into the disposal. An unwelcome thought struck as the mechanism gurgled into action. *Despite his disclaimers to the contrary, Peter must be in love with the unnamed woman.*

Patricia had the oddest sensation that the grinding sound was coming from her chest. She could feel it. It interfered with her breathing. Wincing at the ridiculous idea, she nevertheless drew deep, lifesaving breath into her body.

Her hope of making their marriage work seemed to gurgle down the drain along with their uneaten meal. How could she dream of making their marriage a success if the memory of another woman intruded at their breakfast table and in their bed?

In their bed? Oh, God! Patricia's lips compressed. Her eyes closed against a vision of Peter as he'd been the night before, his eyes glittering with desire, his body hard with passion.

Had Peter's urgency stemmed from a desire to possess his wife, or had he been thinking of the only woman he felt regret over?

Patricia bit her lip to keep from crying out in anguish against the idea of being a substitute lover.

Why should the idea hurt so very much? she chided as the pain expanded inside. Her single goal in agreeing to the union had been to save the company—hadn't it? Not at any time had she entertained the notion of sharing a normal, loving relationship with him. In all fairness, Patricia knew she had no cause for complaint. Peter had promised her fidelity—as long as his physical needs were met. Last night, she had met those needs. Patricia knew, instinctively, that Peter would remain faithful. What more could she ask?

It was at that moment that Patricia realized that she wanted Peter's love as well as his fidelity.

"Patricia?" The sharp edge to Peter's tone pierced her misery. "Is something wrong?"

Yes, something is terribly wrong, Patricia answered in weary silence, shivering as the truth exploded inside her head. I'm in love with a man who *regrets* another woman.

"Patricia!" Peter's tone edged toward impatience.

She had to respond but, hurting from unwelcome awareness, how? Cool composure was a familiar, comforting cloak. Patricia wrapped herself in it with an ease that years of practice had made nearly perfect.

"I'm sorry, I was deep in thought." Not a hint of emotion ruffled her steady tone. "Had you spoken to me before?"

"Several times." His gaze direct and not altogether believing, Peter got to his feet and walked slowly to her. "I asked if there was something wrong." His gaze probed her face, searching for a crack in the glacial mask. The only crack came in the form of a brittle smile.

"No, of course not," she denied, moving away from him to gather the dishes remaining on the table. "What could be wrong?"

What indeed? Peter thought wearily, watching her load the dishes into the dishwasher. For a moment, he had hoped that Patricia was experiencing old-fashioned feminine jealousy, so quiet and withdrawn had she become after his mention of another woman. *I should have known better,* he jeered bitterly to himself. *Had*

I actually dared hope I had found the perfect ice chisel? Dream again, Vanzant.

"So, have you decided what you'd like to do today?" Patricia's overly bright tone ended Peter's reverie.

"Yeah." Peter worked at keeping the disappointment he was feeling out of his voice. He smiled and tried to maintain his laconic tone. "I want to go to the office."

And get away from me for a while? Patricia silently finished for him. "I really don't think we can do that, Peter," she said aloud.

"No, not here in Philadelphia," he agreed, thoughtfully. "But," he went on as inspiration struck, "I see no reason why we can't go to New York and expedite the closing of my office there."

The newly purchased luggage was put to use much sooner than either Patricia or Peter had thought it would be.

Against her better judgment, Patricia found herself seated beside Peter in his custom-appointed Mercedes, en route to New York City, some two hours after he'd made the suggestion. The deciding factor for Patricia had been his use of the plural: "I see no reason why *we* can't go to New York."

When did you take out your subscription to the foolish-women-of-the-world club? Patricia asked herself scathingly as she stared sightlessly through the side window. *Peter Vanzant had not acquired the dubious title of lady-killer by being an average Joe Nobody,* she reminded herself. *And, after his performance last night, it would appear that I am the lady currently at the top of his kill list!*

A wry smile touched Patricia's lips as she realized that her thoughts weren't too far off the mark. Being made love to by Peter Vanzant was such an all-encompassing experience, it could be likened to the loss of the individual self.

The consideration terrified Patricia. She had witnessed her mother's surrender of self to the careless hands of a womanizer. She had suffered the mortification of her own self-esteem at the altar of a man's ego. She would have to be a blithering idiot to consciously offer herself, in the form of her love, to yet another user of women.

No, Patricia decided, withdrawing more deeply into her figurative cloak of ice. She would not allow herself to love Peter Vanzant.

You, my big-mouthed friend, are being well and truly frosted. Uncertain if he had spoken the thought aloud or not, Peter slanted a glance at

Patricia. He swallowed a sigh at the sight of her averted face. *So much for truth and honesty,* he mused cynically. *Now what?* Releasing his grip on the wheel, Peter rubbed the back of his neck with one hand. At that moment, he had no idea how to proceed with his wife.

When Patricia had brought the subject of his reputation with women into their discussion, Peter had genuinely believed she would appreciate complete honesty from him. What point would have been served by denying his previous life-style? he asked himself, frowning at the highway in front of him.

Previous life-style? The phrase echoed in Peter's mind, then faded. Incredible! Peter had to fight to keep from laughing aloud. Peter Vanzant, the arrogant lover on the go, had been shot down in flames, not by a fiery temptress, but by a laser glance from the glacial gray eyes of a lady encased in ice.

And the ice was back. The freeze was on. The glimpse of warmth Patricia had revealed to him had disappeared like a ray of sunlight blocked by a dark snow cloud.

Patricia's warmth had been fleeting, yet, within that relatively short period of time, she had unwittingly exposed her true nature to him.

Peter wanted the true Patricia back. She was his. He had broken through her protective coating of ice once. He would just have to do it again.

Determined, Peter pressed his lips into a straight line as he advised himself to choose a more effective chisel.

Peter's condo, with its panoramic view of Central Park, was breathtakingly beautiful. Patricia disliked it on sight. It wasn't the color scheme of rich browns, stark white and the occasional splash of vibrant melon. Patricia thought the shades blended perfectly, offering an ambience of welcome. Nor was it the artwork that enhanced the overall theme, or even the art-deco pieces that decorated the low tables and wide mantel. No, the one and only thing about the place Patricia disliked was the lingering evidence of a woman's residency.

And the evidence was there. Patricia recognized it at once—any perceptive woman would have. And, against her will, she deeply resented those subtle feminine touches—even as she grudgingly admired the unknown woman's taste.

"Well, what do you think?" Peter asked as they returned to the living room after a tour of the spacious, two-story apartment. He had come to a halt at the wide expanse of undraped window. With his back to the light, his face was shadowed, unreadable.

Circling the room, her fingers lightly brushing objects, surfaces, Patricia flicked a glance at him and as quickly glanced away. Unbidden, her secretary's initial description of him whispered through her mind.

He's dark all over. Hair, eyes, skin. And he has this dark, brooding look. Delicious.

Patricia's glance flickered over him again. Oh, yes, she silently concurred with Donna's account. He is dark, all over. Patricia had had visual proof of his darkness. And he can, at will, assume a definite look of brooding. Peter had immobilized her with that look several times. Delicious? A tremor invaded Patricia's spine. Her lips and tongue could give testimony to how very delicious Peter Vanzant was.

The tremor in Patricia's spine intensified. Donna, in her awe of Peter, had likened him to a god. No, Patricia mutely denied. Peter was no god... But he was the closest thing to it she ever hoped to meet. And, as everybody plainly knew, mere female mortals were not permitted to love gods, not even of the closest-thing variety. One was only allowed to worship from afar. Or one got badly burned in the process.

"No opinion?" Peter's deceptively smooth drawl drew Patricia from the realm of fantasy. "No comment?"

The badly burned Patricia spun to face him. "I'm sorry. I was, ah, into my thoughts. What was the question?" She wasn't positive, but she thought he sighed.

"I was asking what you thought of the place." A lazy sweep of his arm encompassed the apartment. There was nothing at all casual about his taut stance.

"It's fabulous."

"But?" Peter nudged, picking up on her unspoken thoughts.

"But..." Patricia's voice faded. There wasn't a force on earth strong enough to make her admit to her ambiguous feelings. "But nothing," she added lamely.

"Which equates to—you don't like it." Peter's shrug didn't quite make it. Though masked, his disappointment shimmered in the space separating them.

"I didn't say that!" she protested.

"You didn't have to say it," he retorted.

Patricia took an impulsive step toward him. "Peter, I—"

"Don't concern yourself." He cut her off harshly. "I've already decided to sell it." His lips curved, not very pleasantly. "Even though we'll only be in the city for a few days, I can book us into a hotel if you prefer."

"But that would be ridiculous!" Patricia exclaimed, ever mindful of expenses. "Why spend money for a hotel room when we can stay here?"

"Money is not the point, Patricia." If anything, Peter's body tautened even more, almost as if he had been insulted. "I can afford a hotel room for as long as I like. But I have work to do here. I can't afford the distraction of a dissatisfied wife."

No almost about it with Patricia—she was insulted! "I beg your pardon, Mr. Vanzant," she said in the coldest tone she could manage. "I also beg to remind you of the fact that I have not murmured a word of dissatisfaction. What I believe I said was, the apartment is fabulous—" her smile was colder than her voice "—hardly a comment of dissatisfaction." She walked to within inches of him, freezing him with a glance. "Furthermore, rather than distracting you from your work, I had actually planned to offer you

my assistance." Furious, she planted her hands
on her slim hips and glared at him. "Now you
can do your damned work by yourself. *I'm* going shopping."

Nine

Peter locked the door to his midtown Manhattan office for the last time late on Saturday afternoon. His small staff had departed at noon Friday, to go on to the positions Peter had had a hand in securing for them. His desk was clear, all accounts closed. The consultancy firm of Vanzant, Inc. was no more.

For a moment, Peter stared at the door that bore his name in gold script, then he turned and strode to the nearby elevator. The elevator car was empty. Peter sighed and slumped against the wall. He was tired, which in itself was irritating—Peter was never tired. He wanted a shower and a long nap—or twelve solid hours of restful sleep. But he had a final appointment. He was to meet with his realtor at a watering hole on Lexington Avenue in ten minutes. Peter would be late. But it didn't matter, the man would wait. He had a buyer itching to own the uptown condo.

Peter leaned back in the cracked seat of the cab as it made its slow journey across town. It was raining hard, and traffic was a driver's nightmare. Peter didn't care. The gray, oppressive sky and pouring rain fit perfectly with his mood. And his mood was a direct result of the cold war that had existed between him and Patricia since the night of their arrival in New York four days ago.

Peter had slept alone every one of those four nights. And, since he left the apartment very early every morning, and Patricia retired to the guest room very early every night, Peter had seen little of his wife who was not really a wife. Other than her promise to go shopping, he hadn't the vaguest idea how Patricia had filled the long days.

Patricia had closed herself to him. Peter had spent an inordinate amount of time during the previous four days racking his mind for a way to melt her formidable resistance. The few methods he had tried had been met with icy rejection.

Had he actually attempted to buy her? Peter smiled cynically. Yes, he had. Gazing at the mesmerizing back-and-forth slash of the cab's windshield wipers, Peter recalled the two conversations of any length he and Patricia had engaged in. The first had come directly after she'd made her announcement about going shopping...

"You'll need some money," he'd said, reaching for his billfold.

"Don't you dare." Patricia's softly pitched voice was frigid with affront. "I'm perfectly capable of paying for any items I might want to buy."

Ignoring the warning in her tone, Peter had withdrawn several bills of high denomination. "You paid for the suitcase I used today," he'd said reasonably, holding the money out to her. "Let this shopping trip be on me." Dredging up a teasing smile, he had tried to ease the strain between them. "Buy yourself a wildly expensive dress and I'll take you to an elegant restaurant for dinner."

Patricia didn't respond to his smile. She did respond to his offer—coldly.

"You can take your money and...eat it." She was shaking with an inner fury Peter didn't understand, until she continued. "I am not one of your *women*, to be appeased by gifts for services rendered."

Peter got mad. Later he realized he shouldn't have, but by then the damage had been done. "You're right, you're not one of my women." The glance he'd swept over her had been dismissive. "I've never had a woman worth this much money for one night of her *services*." Frustrated, angry, he had thrown the bills at her.

Peter had wished immediately that he could retrieve the stinging insult, for the effect on Patricia was shocking. Pain twisting in his gut, he had watched the color drain from her face and her eyes darken. Gone was the glacial gray, in its place was opaque charcoal. She looked wounded by his verbal thrust; he felt her pain to the depths of his being.

Yet her reaction was even more shocking. Her eyes wide, shimmering with a glaze of tears she refused to acknowledge, Patricia raised trembling fingers to the buttons on her silk shirt.

"What are you doing?" Peter's tone had grown harsh from remorse.

"Preparing to earn my *keep*." Though steady, her voice had been so low Peter could barely discern the emphasis she'd placed on the last word.

"Patricia," he had begun impatiently, "you don't..." All the moisture dried in his throat as the vibrant teal-blue shirt gaped open, revealing a lacy bra and an expanse of satiny skin from the blue lace to the waistband of her slacks. The excitement inside him coiled tightly.

"I know I don't," she had responded to his unfinished rebuke as she unfastened the slacks and slid them down her legs. "But I will." Stepping out of the slacks, she kicked them aside.

Peter had known he should stop her, reassure her, yet he had merely stood there, feeling the heat rise in his body, while she shrugged out of the shirt, then the bra, then the sheer pantyhose that encased her slender legs. Nude, Patricia was a temptation Peter was unequal to. Nude and defiant, her spine straight, her smoky gaze direct, she presented a challenge he was beyond refusing.

His gaze tangling with hers, Peter had torn the clothes from his body. Then, with an arrogance even *he* hadn't realized he was capable of, he had reached for her the instant he was as naked as she. Oddly, the coolness of her skin against his fingers increased the fire roaring through him. Crushing her lips with his, Peter had thrust his tongue into her mouth as he bore her to the floor.

Patricia didn't resist. It was his undoing. There, next to the twenty-dollar bills littering the plush carpet, Peter had obeyed the dictates of unbridled desire by thrusting deeply into the velvety warmth of her body. Reason suspended, he had driven himself, and her, to the very edge of sanity. Rushing, rushing, he drove on, electrified by her fiery response, until, his body slick with sweat, he felt Patricia tighten around him. The sweet cascade of her shudders pushed Peter over the crest of exquisite release.

Awed by the magnitude of the experience, Peter had wanted to hold her, caress her, thank her, then make love to her again. But, even as he parted his lips to convey the pleasure she had given him, Patricia pushed him away then rose to her feet.

"Where are you going?" he had asked blankly, unable to believe she hadn't been as affected by the glorious union as he had.

"I need a bath." Averting her eyes, she walked around him, heading for the stairs. "You can keep the money," she went on in a tone so devoid of life it sent a chill down his spine. "Your *women* get paid. Services from a wife are included with the marriage ceremony.''

Sitting naked on the floor, Peter had accepted her barbs as earned. He had hurt her—cruelly hurt her. But he had hurt himself more.

I need a bath. Her flatly voiced statement pounded inside his head. *I need a bath.* It was as though his lovemaking had dirtied her.

The windshield wipers sang their swishing song. Peter didn't hear it. The driven rain splattered against the side window. Peter didn't see it for the fine mist clouding his eyes.

Strain. Raising a hand, he massaged the bridge of his nose, telling himself the mist in his eyes was caused by the strain of reading too many documents and too little sleep. Not even to himself would Peter admit the pain he'd felt at Patricia's rejection of him—and his money. The bills he had thrown at her still littered the carpet beneath the window in the apartment. He had made a silent vow that the paper would rot before he *stooped* to pick them up.

The second conversation he'd had with Patricia had been shorter and even more painful. The brief exchange had occurred that very morning as Peter was about to leave the apartment for his office. He had opened the door and had taken a step into the corridor when Patricia called to him.

"I'd like a word with you, Peter."

A sensation of dread had unfurled in Peter's stomach at her formal tone. Stepping back into the room, he'd closed the door quietly before turning to glance up at her.

Patricia was standing at the top of the stairs on the second level of the apartment. Peter's throat had gone dry at the sight of her. Unlike the sheer nightgown and peignoir she'd worn on their wedding night, the robe she had on completely concealed her slim, rounded body from his hungry gaze. And yet, though her bearing was regal, her face devoid of warmth or expression, Peter thought her the most beautiful and seductive sight imaginable.

Aching, inside, outside, Peter arched one dark brow in question. "And that word is?"

"Divorce," Patricia said distinctly.

Stunned, Peter had simply stared at her. Attempting to conceal his feelings of desperation, he had said tauntingly, "My dear Patricia, we have been married exactly one week today. Even celebrities endure longer than that."

"Celebrities have their public to consider," she'd shot back at him. "I do not. I am leaving for home this afternoon. I plan to consult with my lawyer Monday morning." Her gaze froze him to the floor. "I just wanted you to know. That's all I have to say."

"How kind of you." Peter's tone was every bit as cold as hers. "Now you can listen to what I have to say." Masking the fury tightening every muscle in his body, he'd sauntered to the foot of the short staircase. His dark eyes pinned her to the landing. "Unless you want to lose your grandfather's precious company, you will wait until I'm ready to return to Philadelphia. And you will also forget your plan to consult with your lawyer—Monday or any other day." He'd paused and narrowed his eyes. "I now own stock equal to your own," he'd warned. "I have the power to destroy the single thing you love most in this damned world. And I will—" he'd smiled, rather nastily, "—unless you are very nice to me." Spinning away, he had slammed out of the apartment before she'd had a chance to respond.

Unless you are very nice to me. Wonderful. Peter grimaced with self-disgust. Over eight hours had elapsed since he had issued the threat. Peter had spent every one of those hours wondering if Patricia was still at the apartment or, after consigning him to hell, had returned to Philadelphia.

"Here ya are, buddy," the cabbie called over his shoulder as he brought the car to a swishing halt in front of the bar and grill.

It was Saturday. It was late in the day. It was raining. And, upon stepping inside the smoky bar, Peter decided that every other person in New York was thirsty, and was quenching that thirst in that particular bar. Getting from the door to where his real-estate agent was sitting at a minuscule table at the back of the room was like attempting to break through the Miami Dolphins' defensive line—sans protective gear. But, using his shoulders ruthlessly, Peter finally made it.

"You look wet, tired and in need of liquid fortification." The agent greeted Peter with a grin.

"Correct on all three," Peter admitted, grasping the man's hand briefly before dropping into a chair.

"Sorry to say there's nothing I can do about the first two." The agent grinned. "But I have the third covered." A flick of his hand indicated the glass filled with amber liquid on the table in front of Peter.

"I always did think you had your priorities straight." Peter tilted the glass in salute. "Thanks, friend." Bringing it to his lips, he downed half the contents of the glass. "Whoa!" Peter breathed as the Scotch burned a trail down the back of his throat. "I think I might live now."

"I felt the same way when I got here," the agent said, an understanding smile tipping up the corners of his full lips. "Ready to talk about selling your place now?"

"Not only ready," Peter said, "but eager."

One hour later, an agreement reached between them, Peter and the realtor parted company. Peter ordered another drink he really didn't want as he watched the agent fight his way to the door.

While he waited for the harried waitress to bring his whiskey, Peter glanced at his watch. It was time to go home, he thought. Hell, it was long past time. But... He shifted on the hard chair in an effort to get comfortable. He didn't want to go home. Peter even knew why he didn't want to go home.

As long as he stayed away from the apartment, he could almost convince himself that Patricia was still there, waiting for him. It was ironic, really, he mused, sipping disinterestedly on the fresh drink. He had always made it his business to know every detail of any situation that even vaguely concerned him. Yet now, in regards to the most important person to ever concern him, he was consciously hanging back, not wanting to know, afraid to know.

Peter was three-quarters through the whiskey when the conversation from the table behind him registered. He had been aware of the litany of complaints sprouting from the mouths of two men, who were both obviously well into their cups. But the majority of their whining gripes had bounced off Peter's distracted mind. The phrase that filtered through his distraction came from one man, young by the tenor of his voice, to the other, in connection to his wife.

"She says that all I ever think about is sex. But, hell, is it any wonder? She's about as hot as a Popsicle in bed."

Unashamedly, Peter strained to hear what, if anything, the other man would say. He didn't have to wait long.

"Yeah, I know what you mean. Not enough sex has got to be the most common complaint of the average husband."

There was a snorting sound; Peter had no idea and cared less which man made it. Then the first speaker piped up again.

"The damn thing is, she couldn't seem to get enough of me before we were married. Now all I get is excuses. She don't want to hear about my problems at the office or about how worried I am about my job. And she sure isn't offering any tender loving comfort, especially of the bedroom kind."

"I got the same deal," the second man moaned. "But, what are you going to do? Life's a bitch, and then you marry one."

Wrong! The denial rang inside Peter's head, drowning out the continuing grind from the two men. *They are dead wrong,* he thought, disgust welling inside. *Most people get exactly what they ask for, whether consciously or subconsciously.*

Startled by a sudden realization, Peter went still for an instant. Then, spurred by a need to think, he pushed his way through the crowd and out onto the sidewalk. It was still raining. Peter didn't care. Head down, hands jammed into his pockets, he began walking and thinking.

People get exactly what they ask for. Peter repeated the phrase slowly, several times, frowning as he applied the concept to himself and his own situation.

Had he deliberately chosen a woman he believed to be cold, unfeeling, ungiving? He pondered, questioning his motivations. Had he, for numerous reasons, sought a woman he could trust and still feel emotionally safe from? Was he, then, an emotional coward?

A passerby, huddled under an umbrella, shot a startled glance at Peter when he laughed aloud harshly. Peter didn't notice. Plodding through the rain that had settled into a steady fall, he was too intent on looking in to take note of outside influences.

The short burst of laughter signaled Peter's acceptance of his own particular form of cowardice. With wry humor, he accused himself of having been an emotional cripple.

The key that unlocked the door to understanding was the phrase "having been." Peter knew that the man sloshing through the rain was not the same man who had repeated the vows of marriage just one week ago. That man had reasons for seeking out a cold woman.

Ignoring the water dripping from his hair and streaking his face, Peter examined his reasons and reasoning. In regards to his decision to marry, his reasoning was simple. His father had been blunt in his desire for a grandchild, preferably a son, to carry on the Vanzant name. Peter himself had faced the fact that he was not getting any younger. He had also begun thinking along the lines of a family of his own. Added to the thoughts of an heir or heirs, Peter genuinely enjoyed the company of women, in and out of bed, but had grown tired of the change of partners. Marriage had seemed the perfect solution.

And that's where his fear came into the picture. He had seen the effects of the devastation being in love could have on a man. Although Peter had observed those effects on many of his friends and acquaintances, his father remained the prime example. His mother had emasculated his father. Even so, Peter's father continued to love the woman who had betrayed him. Peter had decided early on that he'd never give a woman the opportunity to rob him of his pride and manhood.

Distracted by his thoughts, Peter walked right past the elegant apartment building. A scowl of annoyance darkened his face when he was forced to halt for a red light at the corner. Doing an about-face, he trudged back to the building. Nodding to the obviously curious security man,

Peter moved with ever slowing steps to the elevator.

Had she left or was she waiting?

Doubt and raw fear assailed Peter as he stepped into the elevator. Within the short period of one week, Patricia had become the single most important person in his life, more valuable to him than anything he possessed, including his own life.

The elevator doors swished open. Stepping out, Peter stood stock-still, dripping onto the hallway carpet, drawing out the moment of facing what was or was not behind the door to his apartment.

He had deliberately sought her out, not for her warmth but for her apparent lack of it. He had convinced himself he needed no warmth.

Life's a bitch.

Peter smiled wryly at the memory of the man's woeful assertion. Whereas the man in the bar felt cheated by life, the reverse was true for Peter. Subconsciously, he had sought out a cold woman to take for a wife. A woman who, for all intents and purposes, had little use for the male of the species. A woman who would remain faithful simply because other men did not interest her. A woman who would make no emotional demands upon him, nor expect him to make any like demands of her. In fact, a counterpart of himself.

It was really very funny. But Peter wasn't laughing. By some forgotten instinct, had he chosen Patricia not because she was cold but because she was, like him, hiding behind a facade? Had he secretly longed for the warmth he had come to discover she was capable of? Had he known the truth all along, but refused to recognize it? Peter stood absolutely still as the grain of truth settled into the depths of his consciousness.

Without love, life is barren. In being afraid to love, one loses the true joy of life. And now, when it might prove to be too late, Peter ached to grasp that elusive joy with both his hands and his heart.

Forcing his body into motion, Peter walked hesitantly to the door to his apartment. Dipping a hand into his pants pocket, he drew out a ring of keys and separated one from the jingling cluster. In detached wonder, he stared at the tremor in the long fingers directing the key to the lock.

If there's a patron saint of fools, let him hear me, he prayed silently. *Please, make her be in there.* Peter's hands paused, the key hovering above the lock. Then, squaring his shoulders as if preparing himself for whatever he would find, he thrust the key into the lock and turned the doorknob. His last thought before entering the apartment was *If she's gone, you've gotten exactly what you asked for.*

Where is he? Her movements agitated and uncoordinated, Patricia paused in her circuit of the living room to glance at the clock on the wall above the fireplace. The gold-toned hands had inched forward two minutes since the last time she'd looked.

Her mood shifting back and forth between nervous worry and impatient anger, she dropped wearily into a chair, then immediately sprang up again to prowl the confines of the room once more.

Damn it! she railed in frustration. *Where is he?* The question echoed inside Patricia's head. In a city the size of New York, Peter could be any number of places, with any number of friends or acquaintances—male or female. It was the thought of Peter being with a woman that caused her bouts of nervous worry and impatient anger. Because, when push came to shove, Patricia had finally admitted to herself that she was irrevocably, and probably forever, in love with her husband.

In her swing around the room, Patricia's stiff-legged stride brought her close to the wide window. Glancing down, she came to an abrupt halt, gaze fastened on the green bills scattered over the chocolate-brown carpet. As she stared at the money, a sigh of regret whispered through her lips. She had hurt Peter with her refusal to accept money from him. For all his show of anger, Patricia had caught the glimpse of pain he'd felt.

But she had felt pain, too. Peter had inflicted a stunning blow with his reference to her minimal *services*! It was only later, after the fact, that Patricia acknowledged Peter's insult for what it really was—a retaliation against the pain of rejection.

Warmth suffused Patricia's body as her gaze drifted from the green paper to the spot on the carpet where Peter had taken her. And *taken* was the only word that applied. Of course, in all honesty, Patricia admitted to herself that she had taken as greedily from him as he had from her.

Staring at the floor, Patricia envisioned the scene and felt again the searing heat of sensuality. Never had she dreamed she was capable of such abandonment! But if her response to Peter the night before had been a surprise, her hunger for him the following afternoon had been a shocking awakening. And the near-constant craving her body had felt during the emptiness of the past three days had taught Patricia much about herself. She wanted Peter. She longed to feel the fullness of him inside her, loving her, if only with his magnificent body.

Where is he? Sighing softly, Patricia tore her gaze from the carpet to stare out the window. Peter was angry with her—and very likely disgusted. And, she thought bleakly, he had cause for both his anger and disgust. In her initial reaction, she had literally hurled the word *divorce* at him.

Over the days that followed the money incident, days of silence and tension between them, Patricia had come to the decision that they must separate before they tore each other apart emotionally. She had acted on her decision that morning. Peter's reaction had first angered her, then frightened her, then made her think. She had been furious at his arrogance. She had been frightened by his threat to ruin her company. And then she had thought about living the rest of her life without him—with or without the company. Amazingly, after only one week with him, the prospect of not being with Peter instilled an emptiness inside Patricia that was immobilizing.

And so, after three days of frantically running away from the necessity of facing the truth in wild sprees of shopping, Patricia had spent that entire day taking a long, hard look at herself. What she saw was not very appealing. For what she saw was a woman who had coldly, deliberately removed herself from the sheer pleasure of life and love in fear of being hurt by both. In the end she had hurt herself more. Securely encased in her protective layer of ice, Patricia realized she could have lived her life and never known the joy to be found in Peter's arms.

Thank God Peter had gone his own arrogant way and decided the issue for her! Patricia thought, kneeling on the floor to pick up the litter of paper Peter had offered to her, she now realized, as a form of peace offering.

And she had thrown his offer in his face, precisely as she had thrown her challenge of a divorce in his face. Staring at the window, Patricia mused on her own stupidity. What, she chided herself, had she expected from him? A meek acceptance of her request for a divorce? Peter? She had to have been out of her mind! Hadn't Peter arrogantly told her he hadn't been able to refuse the challenge she'd presented to him on the day they met?

But Peter was made up of more than arrogance. Peter was laughter and strength, warmth and passion, and a thousand nuances in between. And, during the quiet of that long afternoon, Patricia had come to the realization that she would be completely mad to close him out of her life. Peter had promised her the one thing she had believed impossible for any man to give—his fidelity. How could she now ask for more?

A finger of dread slid down Patricia's spine at the sound of a key being turned in the lock. Drawing a deep breath, she eased around to face her future . . . or her past. Her fingers curled around the crisp bills in her hand.

His suit coat sodden, his pants legs splattered with dirty water spewn from the tires of passing cars, Peter looked more like a down-at-heels panhandler than the arrogant, self-confident man he was. A shocked gasp burst from Patricia's tight throat at the incongruous sight he made.

"Good heavens, Peter!" she cried. "What happened to you?" Without thought she rushed to him.

"I walked." Raising a hand, he brushed at the dripping strands of hair laying across his forehead.

"From the office?" Moving around him, she tugged at the sleeves of his jacket as he shrugged it from his shoulders.

"No." The jacket off, he bent to tug his shoes and clinging socks from his feet. "I had a meeting at a bar on Lexington. I walked from there," he explained in a tired tone she had never before heard from him.

A meeting? Patricia repeated silently. A meeting with whom? Hesitant to ask, and not sure she wanted to know, she stood by feeling both useless and helpless as he yanked the once pristine white shirt from his trousers.

"Not interested in knowing who I had the meeting with?" Glancing at her, Peter arched his brows in a pale imitation of his former imperious expression of query. When she failed to respond immediately, a resigned look flickered over his face. "Yeah," he muttered harshly, moving to the staircase.

"Who did you meet with?" Patricia had to force the question past the dread tightening her throat.

Peter paused with one foot on the bottom stair. "I had an appointment with my realtor." He didn't look at her.

"In a bar?" she asked skeptically.

Peter turned his head to level a dull-eyed stare at her. "I never lie, Patricia. I can't be bothered." A hint of his usual arrogance lanced his tone.

Patricia felt a surge of relief wash through her at the almost normal sound of his voice. She could relate to an arrogant Peter. The Peter who had sounded defeated terrified her. "I haven't accused you of lying," she said, "I merely consider a bar to be a strange place for a meeting."

"Not strange at all," he contradicted, starting up the stairs. "I've sold the apartment," he tossed back, as if the information was of little importance.

"Peter!"

Peter halted on the landing to stare down at her somberly. "I need a hot shower, Patricia. We'll discuss it when I come back down." He turned away again.

"Have you had dinner?"

"I'm not hungry." This time he didn't pause. His dry tone floated down the stairs to her. "I drank my dinner."

Her eyes cloudy with anxious concern, Patricia stared at the empty landing. Then she whirled and rushed into the kitchen. Her movements economical, she started a pot of coffee, then gathered the ingredients for an omelet. While the coffee brewed, she prepared the eggs. She was folding the omelet in the pan when he called to her.

"Patricia."

Before she could reply, he called again, so sharply it startled her.

"Patricia!"

"I'm in the kitchen," she called back, assembling coffee, cups, cream and his food on a large tray. "I'll be there in a—second," she finished faintly as he pushed through the kitchen door.

"What are you doing?" Placing his hands on his hips, Peter swept the scene with a hard-eyed glance before settling his gaze on her.

"I made you some supper," she answered steadily.

"Oh." His hands fell to his sides. "It wasn't necessary." His gaze slid the length of her body, missing nothing, warming considerably as he absorbed the disheveled look of her tousled hair and less than chic appearance in a wraparound denim skirt and a velour pullover. "But I'm glad you did," he went on softly, reaching for the tray.

Feeling messy and unkempt after the thoroughness of his perusal, Patricia smoothed her palms over her hips, then tugged at the hem of her sweater. "I—I stayed inside all day and, ah, didn't bother about clothes." Even as she told herself it wasn't necessary, she defended her careless appearance.

Balancing the tray in his hands, Peter stared at Patricia for a moment. Then he smiled at her for the first time in four days. Patricia had the uncanny sensation that the sun had burst through the kitchen ceiling. "You look beautiful," he said, the smile fading as his eyes warmed.

"Thank you." Patricia felt as though the sun had invaded her body. Moistening her dry lips, she indicated the forgotten tray in his hands. Her voice nearly deserted her when his gaze fastened on her lips. "Your supper will get cold," she said, swallowing roughly.

Peter walked to her, stopping when the edge of the tray indented the soft material over her midriff. His eyes darkened, heating her body to flash point.

"I want to make love with you."

Patricia swayed toward him, catching her equilibrium when the tray dug into her flesh. The situation was ridiculous. It was not the time or place. There were far too many questions to ask, answers to be given. Patricia suddenly didn't care. Raising her hands, she slid her fingers over his.

"After you've eaten your supper," she promised in a tone that spoke of her own hunger.

Ten

Ten

___

Peter's eyes darkened and for a moment Patricia half hoped, half feared he would set the tray aside and take her right there in the kitchen. Then, smiling ruefully, he backed away from her. "You were planning to take this into the living room?"

"Yes." Patricia was slightly amazed at the quivery sound of her voice. "I thought you'd be more comfortable there."

Peter hesitated a moment longer then he swung around and pushed through the door. He headed for the sofa in front of the cleverly designed electric fireplace and was midway to it when he stopped abruptly. Following closely behind him, Patricia nearly plowed into him.

"Peter, what is..." her voice trailed away as she noted the object of his intent scrutiny. He was staring at the spot on the floor where he'd flung the handful of bills.

"I—I picked up the money," she blurted out starkly. "You may have it back if you want it." Patricia regretted her offer the instant it was out of her mouth. Would she never learn? she berated herself, watching as a fine tremor rippled the length of his strong back.

"I'm sorry."

They spoke simultaneously then fell silent. Observing him closely, Patricia felt a stab of compassion when he winced as his gaze shifted to the spot on the carpet where he had made such forceful, exciting love to her three days ago.

"You have nothing to be sorry for," Peter said in a tone gritty with emotion. "I insulted you, then added injury to that insult by my actions." Turning to face her fully, he said softly, "I promised I'd never deliberately hurt you, and then broke my promise less than twenty-four hours later." His expression exposed a vulnerability that tugged at Patricia's heart. "And all I can say is, I am sorry."

"And so am I," she responded contritely. Faced with his vulnerability and honesty, she could not offer him less. "I provoked you, Peter. You unknowingly stabbed at an old wound and I reacted stupidly. I am more to blame than you are."

"Patricia..." Peter took a step toward her and was again halted by the tray in his hands.

"Your supper's getting cold, Peter," she said practically, reminded of the food on the tray between them.

Peter frowned. "You can't toss out a statement like that then not explain it." He glanced down at the food then back at her. "We can talk while I eat." His movements decisive, he turned to walk to the sofa.

After they were seated side by side on the long sofa, Peter sliced his fork through the omelet, speared the severed piece and slid it into his mouth.

"I'm eating." As a prompt, it was less than subtle. A hint of a smile quirked his lips. "And it's delicious, too. You make a mean omelet, Patricia."

His compliment eased the tension that had gripped her at his request for an explanation. "Thank you," she murmured, inordinately pleased by his approval of her cooking ability.

"You're welcome," he said, slicing into the egg again. "What old wound did I stab at to make you react stupidly?" Popping the portion into his mouth, he chewed with obvious enjoyment and leveled a no-nonsense, "let's have it" look at her.

Patricia smoothed her palms over her skirt and felt the outline of the bills she'd stuffed into her pocket when she'd heard his key in the door. The feel of the money had more to do with nudging her into speech than his expression.

"My father was always giving my mother things," she began slowly, "and money." Her lips twisted wryly. "It was really pitiful, considering the money was rightfully hers to begin with."

Though he continued to wolf down the food, Peter's eyes narrowed thoughtfully. "Go on," he urged when she paused.

"It was conscience money and gifts," she said bitterly. "He was pandering to mother's love of clothes and her taste for exquisite things."

"Why conscience money?" Sensing the reason for Patricia's glacial manner, Peter shot the question at her. His shot hit home.

"Because he was sleeping with every beautiful woman he could talk into bed with him," Patricia shot back. "Apparently, he was a very good talker."

"Hmm." Sipping his coffee, Peter gazed at her over the rim of the cup. "And that gave you the belief that all men are faithless?" he asked with deceptive calm. Inside, Peter was beginning to believe he had found a kindred spirit.

Patricia sighed as she realized that Peter was not going to rest until he'd heard her entire history. She moistened her dry lips, feeling a curl of response when his gaze shifted to her mouth.

"My father was the beginning," she went on in a raw tone. "The end was a young man in my second year of college."

Peter felt a shaft of hot jealousy; had he really believed Patricia had never been in love? Yes, he really had. The knowledge that she had cared deeply for some insensitive man filled him with both anger and compassion. "You were in love with him?" Peter decided the question was possibly the hardest he had ever asked.

"Yes." Patricia's tone conveyed a sense of defeat.

Replacing the cup on the tray, Peter squashed an urgent desire to take her protectively in his arms. Along with the desire to protect was the desire to possess. Not trusting his resistance to the latter, he denied himself the former.

"And?" he prompted tightly, knowing it all had to be said before she could regroup her defenses and close him out by freezing up again.

"He used me." Patricia's lips curved cynically. "I was a virgin with a reputation. I was considered impossible to get." Her voice was now hoarse with emotion. "He was out to bag a trophy."

"The bastard." Peter's voice was hard.

"Exactly," Patricia agreed wholeheartedly. "A man."

Alarm flared in Peter's head. Damn! He had to stop her. "Patricia," he began, but she went on as if he hadn't spoken.

"He offered me money, too." As if suddenly realizing what she'd said, Patricia froze. She had never told another soul about the young man's offer to pay her! She'd been so humiliated that she had buried the memory of it, along with the budding hint of sensuality he had aroused.

"And I revived the pain by offering you money," Peter said tiredly. "No wonder you reacted as you did."

At the sound of weariness in his tone, Patricia forced the chill from *her* tone. Peter was not at fault. She could not punish him for another man's crime. With the realization that she had been doing exactly that—punishing all men for the pain she'd suffered at the hands of two thoughtless males—Patricia felt a stab of regret for all the years she had wasted in bitterness.

"You were not to blame, Peter," she insisted.

"I know." Peter's smile was strained. "But, you see, *I* was reacting to past grievances also." With a sigh he set the tray aside, then slumped back against the sofa cushions. "When I offered the money to you I was following my father's example—if unconsciously."

"I don't un—"

"As I suspect you know," he cut her off, "my mother is a faithless wife." His smile reflected all the bitterness Patricia had harbored for years. "And still my father continues to love her. He indulges her, lavishes money and things on her, in the futile hope of buying her fidelity."

"You love your father very much, don't you?" Patricia asked softly.

"Yes." Peter sighed again. "I love my mother, too—even while I hate her for what she's made of him."

Understanding dawned in Patricia, and she impulsively moved yet nearer to him. "And you were determined not to allow a woman to do the same to you?" she asked quietly.

"Yes." Peter gazed narrowly at the floor beneath the window. "But I hadn't realized how uncivilized I'd become in the process. I am sorry, Patricia," he murmured, vulnerable once again. "Sorry for my insensitivity, my savagery and my threat."

Having forgotten it, Patricia frowned. "Threat?"

"This morning," he reminded her. "I was bluffing. I threatened to ruin your company in an attempt to regain control of both you and the entire situation in true macho style." He grimaced. "I sold this place today." He indicated the apartment with a negligent wave of one hand. "We're going home tomorrow."

"All right," she agreed, acting on an impulse to move still closer to him until their sides touched from hip to shoulders.

Peter stiffened and clenched his hands, as if to control the need to haul her into his arms. "I won't fight you if you decide to meet with your lawyer," he said tersely.

"I've canceled the appointment, Peter." Raising her hand spontaneously, she smoothed her fingers over the lines of strain etching his lips and smiled when he inhaled sharply.

"I ate every bit of my supper, Patricia," he whispered, leaning forward to brush her lips with his warm mouth. "I want the dessert you promised me."

"Then take it," she whispered invitingly, gliding the tip of her tongue along the rough edge of his bottom teeth.

Peter reacted like dry tinder that is touched by spark. A deep growl vibrating in his throat, he crushed her trembling mouth beneath his. The flame of his searching tongue ignited a blaze in the deepest reaches of Patricia's body. Flinging pride to the wind, she molded her soft curves to the muscles in his arms and shoulders, chest and legs, and returned his kiss with a stunning passion.

With a sweeping move Peter had her on her back, his body pinning hers to the plush cushions. His hands crushed the velour sweater as they cupped her breasts. A low moan escaped her lips when he found the hardening crests.

"This is no good," he said, his voice raw. Pulling his head back, he looked at his hands, then his gaze captured hers. "I want to see you. I want you to see me."

"Yes." Lifting her lowered lashes, Patricia let him see the desire in her eyes. "But the bedroom's so far away."

A smile tipped the corners of his lips. "We know the carpet's soft," he murmured, sliding his hands to the hem of her sweater. "And only a short drop from here." Grasping the material, he slid it up her body to expose her lace-covered breasts. The crests were sharply outlined against the sheer lace. Breathing deeply, he lowered his head. A cry of pleasure was wrenched from her throat as he gently tasted one taut bud with his tongue.

"Will it be the carpet or right here?" Peter asked tightly, feeling sensation unfurl inside him as he wet the lacy material of her bra with his lips and tongue. When she didn't respond immediately he nipped at the bud with his teeth. "Hurry, Patricia," he muttered urgently. "I'm not wearing shorts, and the zipper's playing hell with some very tender skin."

"I'm sorry!" she gasped, shaking her head to clear it of the mist of passion. His rakish smile eased her concern.

"Don't be," he said teasingly, heaving his body from hers. Kneeling on the floor, he drew her down next to him. "Actually, it hurts real good." Encircling her wrist with his fingers, he drew her hand to the section under discussion.

For an instant Patricia froze, then, intrigued by a sense of power, she stroked the material that prevented her from touching his flesh.

"That does it!" Peter exclaimed in a strangled voice. Pulling her with him, he sprang to his feet.

Within seconds their clothes lay scattered on the floor. Naked and aroused, he stood before her, his eyes devouring her quivering body. Then, sliding his arms around her, he drew her with him to the floor. His mouth seared over her body like a finger of fire. The tension singing along her nerves tautened her body and arched it in sweet offering to his daring mouth. Peter accepted her gift greedily, tasting the sweetness of her feminine honey.

"Peter! Peter!" Patricia cried out against the exquisite torture.

A shuddering response shook his body at the sound of his name on her lips and the feel of her hands tugging on his shoulders in a silent plea. Obeying her mute command, he slid his body up the fevered length of hers. Peter exhaled on a long sigh as he joined her body to his.

"Melt around me, my lady ice," he whispered, molding his parted lips to hers. "Warm me with your inner heat."

Patricia didn't feel the resistance of the hard floor beneath her. Nor did she notice the slight abrasion of the carpet fibers against her tender skin. Peter was with her, inside her, making her a part of him, becoming a part of her. Her senses spinning, Patricia fantasized that there was a mystical importance to the act that would in some way bind them together in reality. When Peter cried her name at the exact instant joy exploded deeply within her, she almost believed the fantasy could become a reality.

Patricia woke with a start. It was still dark. It was still raining. Something had pulled her from the bliss of slumber—but what? Muffling a yawn with her palm, she shifted from her side to her back. A faint frown drew a line on her brow at the sight that met her sleepy-eyed gaze.

Fully dressed in casual slacks and a bulky knit sweater, Peter was standing at the end of the bed, neatly arranging a suit coat on a hanger. Her frown deepened as she watched him hang the jacket inside the garment bag they had purchased the previous Monday.

"What are you doing?" Her question was almost lost inside a yawn.

In the act of reaching for another jacket, Peter glanced up, a tentative smile on his lips. "Packing." Picking up a hanger, he draped the jacket over it. "I told you I wanted to go home today."

"Today?" Patricia sliced a glance at the window. "It's still night!" Memory flooded back and she looked around in confusion. She had drifted off to sleep in his arms on the living-room floor. Yet now she was in a bed—Peter's bed! His soft chuckle captured her scattered thoughts.

"It is today." He glanced at the watch on his wrist. "Six-fifteen, to be exact."

"Oh . . ." Patricia's voice trailed away, then came back a little stronger. "How did I get in here?"

Peter had turned to walk to the closet. He slanted a wry look at her over his shoulder. "I carried you." His lips curved with amusement. "You were so deeply asleep, you didn't flutter as much as an eyelash." A smile of male satisfaction twitched his lips. "Making love—twice—really relaxes you," he said teasingly, strolling back to the foot of the bed.

Warmth suffused Patricia's body from her ankles to her hairline. His teasing evoked an image of their lovemaking on the living-room carpet. They had been so hungry for one another that once had not been enough to quench their appetites. Feeling his gaze sear over her, she drew the covers more closely around her.

"Shy, Patricia?" Peter chided softly, moving around the end of the bed to sit beside her on the edge of the mattress. "After last night?"

Patricia missed the note of uncertainty underlying his low voice. "Yes, this is all, ah, rather new to me," she said, lowering her gaze.

His eyes growing dark with tenderness, Peter stroked her warm cheek with one hand. "I know," he murmured, then added encouragingly, "we still have a lot to learn about each other. Last night was a start in the right direction." Trailing his hand down her throat, he paused at the edge of the covers she held against her. "I know every inch of your beautiful body, wife. I've touched, tasted and made love to it." With a gentle tug, he drew the cover away. "I enjoy the husbandly pleasure of seeing you as other men have not. Please don't litter our path to mutual understanding by unnecessary inhibitions now."

Though Patricia's body quivered, she forced herself to remain still while Peter's gaze drifted slowly over her from her eyes to her toes. The combination of admiration and desire that flared in his eyes as he returned his gaze to hers brought the realization that she was quivering in expectation, not embarrassment.

"You are beautiful," he whispered, bending to kiss the tips of her breasts before raising his mouth to kiss her lips. "And," he added in a darkly sexy voice, "if you're wise, you'll get moving, before I decide to join you in that bed."

Wondering why she opted for being wise, Patricia leaped from the bed to run into the bathroom. Peter's warm laughter followed to send a shiver down her spine.

The drive back to Philadelphia was conducted in near silence. But the quiet was not because they had nothing to say to one another, rather it was because they had too much to say to launch into an in-depth conversation while driving through worsening weather conditions. Rain lashed the windshield, obscuring Peter's vision. Peter broke the silence every few miles with a

muffled curse. Patricia merely hid a smile and
averted her face.

They both sighed with relief when he brought
the car to a splashing stop in the driveway beside
his town house. Even while inside the car, they
could hear the rain pounding on the carport roof.

"We'll leave the bags 'till later," Peter said,
grimacing as a gust of wind swept the rain under
the protective roof. "I think we'll have to make
a dash for the door." Pushing his door open, he
stepped out. Patricia followed his action.

"I'll need my makeup case," she called, hur-
rying toward the back door that led into the
laundry room of the town house.

"Why?" Entering the small room behind her,
Peter pulled the door quietly. "Your skin's like
satin," he murmured, moving close to her. "Why
do you hide it under a layer of cosmetics?"

Patricia paused before opening the door that
led into the kitchen. There was more puzzlement
than compliment in Peter's tone. A tingle set her
nerve endings quivering. Heat invaded her body
as she observed him examining her features. The
heat was fanned into a blaze when his gaze settled on her mouth. In the laundry room? she
thought in startled excitement. The consideration restored her equilibrium and her sense of
humor. She had no idea that Peter felt the ef-

fects of her sensuous smile all the way to the soles of his feet.

"I wasn't trying to hide," she said, her hand on the doorknob. "I was trying to enhance."

Peter leaned forward to brush her parted lips with his. "It's impossible to enhance perfection," he murmured before capturing her mouth with his.

Patricia held onto the doorknob for dear life. As passion leaped between them, she gently pushed against his chest. "In the laundry room, Peter?" She voiced her earlier thought as she turned the knob and pushed open the kitchen door.

"Hurry, wife," Peter whispered at her ear. "We have a lot of communicating to do."

The sight that met Patricia's eyes as she entered the kitchen scattered her thoughts.

"Nicole?" she said blankly.

She was seated at the table, staring morosely into a steaming cup of coffee. She glanced at the sound of her name. "I'm sorry," Nicole said helplessly. "I just couldn't take any more of mother." Against Peter's wishes, she had opted to move home the week before the wedding.

"What did she do?" Peter asked sharply, striding over to his sister.

Nicole gave her brother a bleak smile. "She insisted on doing the smothering-mother routine. She also insisted I see another analyst."

Peter snarled a curse so obscene Patricia gasped with shock. She had heard him swear several times on the drive home, but nothing compared to the expletives that growled from him now. "Peter, really!" she scolded, frowning at his sister's pale face.

"You don't understand." Peter dismissed her chastisement with a shrug. "Nicole went through analysis after the car accident. She doesn't need anyone poking into her mind. She needs time." His broad hand came to rest protectively on his sister's shoulder.

"I see." Patricia studied his fierce expression for a moment. His concern was obvious. Though she had hoped they could resolve their marriage on their return, she accepted the delay. Sitting down opposite Nicole, she said what Peter was hoping to hear from her. "You'll stay here with us, of course."

Nicole couldn't conceal the relief that washed through her, though she did try. "You two have a right to be alone," she demurred. "I don't want to intrude on your privacy."

"Damn it, Nicole!"

"You will not be intruding!"

The protests came simultaneously from Patricia and Peter. Before either one could elaborate, however, Nicole settled the issue.

"Okay, I'll stay. But only until I find someplace else to go." Her tone held a strength and adamance neither Patricia nor Peter cared to challenge.

"That's my girl," Peter approved quietly, his tone revealing how very long he'd waited for the sound of strength from his sister.

"Very well," Patricia said briskly, "that's settled." Then, attempting to ease the sense of strain in the room, she went on. "Now, what about lunch? I'm hungry."

"I'm famished." The glance Peter shot at Patricia reactivated the tingles of response. His dark eyes said plainly that food was not what he was famished for.

It was many hours before Peter got a chance to appease his physical appetite. As Patricia had taken a genuine liking to Nicole, she automatically assumed the responsibility of lifting her spirits out of the depression Peter's mother had cast her into. It was nearing midnight when Patricia finally left the younger woman at the door of her bedroom. As Nicole's mood was noticeably lighter, Patricia went to her own bedroom with a warm feeling of accomplishment. That she went to the room she had occupied before she and Peter left for New York was an uncalculated error. Peter slammed through the connecting door as she was undressing.

"What the hell do you think you're doing?" he demanded, jamming his fists on his hips in blatant masculine challenge.

Patricia blinked in surprise. "I'm preparing for bed." She stated the obvious.

"Not in here," he said imperiously. "From now on you will sleep in *my bed,* with me."

Patricia reacted to his tone in the manner she'd adopted ten years previously; she froze. Unmindful of the fact that she was barely covered by her lacy bra and skimpy panties, she drew herself up to her full height and turned on the ice. "Indeed?" she responded chillingly.

Rather than instilling caution, her tone fired anger in Peter. "You're damned right, indeed." Stepping to her, he curled his fingers around her wrist. "Let's go," he said, indicating his room with a motion of his free hand.

Sheer, unadulterated fury tore through Patricia. *Let's go?* she repeated mutely, glaring at him. *Was this his idea of communication? But of course. What else?* Her thoughts tumbled on. *He's a man, isn't he?* Even as she regrouped the inner core of ice, Patricia felt a stinging pain of disappointment.

"I prefer to sleep in here." Patricia's eyes resembled an ice floe in shadow. "Now—" she yanked her wrist free of his loose grip "—if you will excuse me?" Indicating that she didn't care one way or the other, Patricia turned her back to him. It was a mistake.

Muttering a curse that should have turned the air blue, Peter caught her and swung her up into his arms. "You have presented your damned back to me once too often," he said in a near growl. Striding into his bedroom, he kicked the door shut with his bare heel, then crossed to the wide bed. Ignoring her yelp of fury, he tossed her onto the mattress. "You are my wife," he whispered in an anger-tight voice. "And you will share my bed." He discarded his silky robe with an economy of motion.

Stunned by his actions, Patricia had not moved, but merely stared at him in disbelief. At the sight of his naked, fully aroused body, she attempted to scramble to the far side of the bed. She had hesitated an instant too long. Flinging himself onto the bed beside her, Peter encircled her waist with one arm and tangled his free hand in her hair.

"You're hurting me," she said, seething inside because of his rough treatment—and because of the responsive heat she felt building inside.

"Not yet," he said, his voice husky with passion. Sliding his hand up her rib cage, he released the catch at the front of her bra then captured one breast with his warm hand. "And I won't if you behave."

Behave! Did he think he was speaking to a child? Patricia's fury rose another notch. She ached to scream at him. She ached to hit him. But undermining her anger was the fact that she ached—period. The tips of her breasts ached for his touch. Her mouth ached for his kiss. Her body ached for the fullness of his. Her eyes, shading from cold to smoky gray, betrayed her.

"You want me, Patricia," Peter groaned, gliding his hand down her body. "Admit it."

"I don't," she lied, shivering as his hand moved to tear away the sheer barrier of her panties.

"How much don't you want me?" Peter's mint-scented breath misted her lips an instant before she tasted the mint on his tongue.

This was not resolving anything! Patricia tore her mouth from his as the thought rang in her mind. They already knew they were good together in bed!

"Why are you doing this?" she cried, arching uncontrollably into his maddening touch.

Peter didn't feel confident enough with her to admit how the mention of his mother's name had affected him. During the afternoon and throughout the evening, while Patricia worked at reassuring Nicole, he had been tormented by thoughts of his father, the man enslaved to a faithless woman. Now, Peter felt consumed by the need to define his relationship with his own wife.

"Because I've been wanting you all night," he finally responded, giving her half the truth. "And you want me," he insisted, finding her breast with his lips, "don't you?"

"Yes!" Patricia gasped as exquisite pleasure radiated from her breast to each tiny nerve ending.

"Yes," he repeated in a husky murmur, stroking her silkiness. "And you belong to me, don't you?" he growled, before drawing intricate designs around her navel with the tip of his tongue.

"No!" The word *belong* chilled her mind, if not her body.

"You will," he vowed, moving between her thighs.

Then she gave her body to him, wildly calling his name with the power of her shuddering release. His skin was wet, his own voice was hoarse as he cried her name with the pulsating release of his life force.

The experience was mind-altering in its effect upon Peter. Drawing harsh gulps of air into his body, he levered himself onto the mattress beside Patricia. Never had a sexual encounter left him with quite the same feeling. Peter hesitated to even think the word awe, yet that was exactly what he was feeling. It wasn't until his breathing had evened to near normal that Peter became aware of Patricia, still shuddering next to him. Rolling to his side, he curled an arm around her waist to draw her close. A sensation too close to panic flared in his mind at the sight of tears trickling down her expressionless face.

"Patricia?"

Patricia barely heard him for the echo of the word *belong* ringing in her mind. Had she really begun to believe in him? What now of his path to understanding? she thought despairingly.

"Patricia, answer me!"

Wrapped inside her own growing fear, Patricia was beyond hearing a corresponding fear in his tone. *He doesn't want a marriage, an equal partnership,* she thought sickly. Peter wants to *own* me. A vision of her father increased the flow of hot tears from her eyes. *No. I can't. I won't expose myself to the hurt and humiliation my mother suffered!* In self-defense, she drew the remnants of her ice cloak around her.

"Patricia, don't," Peter pleaded, brushing her tears away with his fingers. "I swear I didn't mean..."

"I will sleep in your bed, Peter." She spoke softly over his voice. "I will be your wife." Moving her head on the pillow, Patricia stared directly into his eyes. She didn't notice the spasm of pain that moved across his face as he witnessed the absence of life in her eyes. She was too involved with dealing with her own pain. "I will not make a fool of myself by denying I receive satisfaction from having sex with you."

"Patricia!" Peter recoiled as if she had slapped him at her use of the phrase "having sex" instead of "making love." "I want to—"

"You may have the use of my body, Peter," she went on, cutting him off again. "But you will never own it, or me." With unnerving calm, she brushed his arm aside and rose from the rumpled bed. "I'm going to have a shower," she said tonelessly. "And then I'm going to sleep. I must go back to work tomorrow." Not sparing him a glance, she walked from the room.

The three weeks that followed that night were the worst Peter had ever lived through. Patricia shared the company, the house, the bed with him. But she gave nothing of herself. All her warmth was reserved for Nicole, who responded like a flower to a long-overdue rainfall. And, while he was both relieved to note the change in his sister and grateful to Patricia for her part in that change, he couldn't help feeling that he had lost his own chance at finding real contentment.

Patricia lived those weeks in a haze of misery and a whirl of enforced activity. Though she shared his bed each night, Peter had made no intimate move toward her. And the truth was, she longed for his kiss, his touch and the union, if only physical, to be found with him.

At first, because she was disappointed with him, she maintained her anger at him. When anger died for lack of fuel, she told herself to leave, get away from his destructive influence. But it was too late. There was a flaw in her protective core of ice. The chill cloak no longer fit. What good would it do to leave him? she reasoned. She loved him. Separation would not make her love him less. And, if she was destined to be miserable, she decided to be miserable close to him.

The battle that had commenced in the bedroom the night of Peter's and Patricia's return from New York had settled into a cold war. For Nicole's sake, they made polite, and inanely unimportant, conversation when in each other's company. They barely spoke when alone. They worked together. They lived together. They were strangers.

Nicole set the wheels in motion to end the war as unwittingly as she had caused it. It was Friday evening, the end of the third week of strain. It was over the dinner table, the only meal the three ever shared—and that not often.

"I'm leaving tonight." Nicole's statement had the effect of a bomb tossed onto the table.

"Leaving?" Patricia repeated blankly.

"Where are you going?" Peter's voice was just a shade less blank. "Do you have an appointment in the city?" he asked, remembering her mysterious appointments of two months ago.

"No." Nicole shook her head. "I've been in touch with Barbara." She slid a sideways glance at Peter. "She invited me to the ranch."

"Barbara?" Patricia frowned; she had never heard the name mentioned before. "Who's Barbara?"

"A friend," Nicole explained, avoiding her brother's eyes. "We modeled together years ago. She got married last fall. Her husband owns a ranch in Texas, near San Antonio. They've invited me to spend the summer with them. I'm booked on a flight to Houston tonight."

Through dinner, and the ensuing confusion of getting Nicole's already packed things together and into the car, Patricia had the feeling she was being sheltered from something. Nicole candidly answered every one of Patricia's questions, yet the odd feeling persisted up to the minute she and Peter saw Nicole off at the airport. The feeling settled into certainty with Peter's casual parting remark.

"Give Barbara my best, and tell her that I sincerely hope she's happy."

During the drive back to the house, Peter's words and the tone of his voice echoed inside Patricia's mind. The woman, Barbara, had meant something to him. Patricia suddenly knew it as surely as she knew her own name. She also knew why Nicole had avoided Peter's eyes.

When they arrived back at the house, Patricia went straight to the bedroom, fighting weariness, tears and a yawning emptiness inside. Peter entered the room as she was hanging her clothes in the closet. Slipping into a lightweight robe, she turned away and walked into the bathroom. While standing under a warm shower, Patricia told herself she had two options. She could avoid the subject of this faceless Barbara, or she could meet the topic head on. As she dried her body then slid a nightgown over her head, she decided she'd had about enough of avoidance. Perhaps it was time for some genuine communication! Leaving the robe lying on the clothes hamper, she walked back into the bedroom, prepared, if necessary, for a battle royal.

Clad once again in nothing but the silky robe, Peter was standing by the window, his shoulders squared, his expression wary. "I think it's time we..." His voice trailed away as his gaze slowly traveled the length of her body, tantalizingly revealed by the sheer nightgown.

"She was important to you at one time, this friend of Nicole's," Patricia said quickly, before she could change her mind. "Wasn't she?"

Peter's gaze met hers. A fire simmered in the dark depths of his eyes. Still, he answered her with brutal frankness. "Yes. Barbara was one of my—ah—women. The only woman I ever lived with before, and the only one I ever came close to loving."

Having her suspicions about another woman in his apartment confirmed hardly imbued a sense of victory in Patricia. The only comfort she could derive was in his disclaimer.

"You didn't love her?" she asked starkly, tired of evasion and cloudy issues.

"No." The derision in Peter's smile was directed at himself. "I wouldn't allow myself to love her." Obviously he was as tired of evasion as she, for he drew a deep breath, then went on. "I was determined never to love any woman. I could like them, enjoy them, *make love* to them, but never give any one of them the weapon of my love to use against me."

His tone had grown hard, startling Patricia.
Use the weapon of love against him, she repeated to herself, feeling an uncanny sensation in
the pit of her stomach. *But wasn't that exactly
the way she had always felt? Hadn't she been
afraid of handing the weapon of love to another?* A shiver ran a jagged line down her spine
and she jumped when he moved toward her.

"Don't be afraid of me, Patricia, please." Soft
entreaty shimmered on his voice. "I have no desire to hurt you." Coming to a stop in front of
her, he slid a hand into the pocket of his robe.
"I . . . I have a gift for you."

He was so close she could feel the warmth of
his body, smell the familiar minty scent of his
breath. And suddenly, she wanted nothing more
from life than the right to touch his warmth, taste
the freshness of his mouth. The shiver that had
started to shake her inner being became a tremor,
then a quake strong enough to shatter the remaining layer of ice inside her.

"A—a present?" She felt hot and cold and
scared witless. She didn't feel at all like herself;
she felt more like a woman.

"Yes." His movements betraying tension, Peter took a small box from his pocket. He placed
it in her hand so very gently it was as if he were
handing her the most fragile gift imaginable.
"Open it," he ordered when she hesitated.

Her fingers cold, trembling, Patricia carefully lifted the lid from the flat velvet box. Lying on a bed of white satin was a gold ring. Patricia gazed down at the circlet for long moments, then looked up at him in puzzlement.

"It's beautiful," she whispered, "but I don't understand. What is it for? It's too large for my finger and too small for my wrist." She tried to smile and failed. "Peter, what is it for?"

"My nose."

His quiet but certain tone, the half hopeful, half fearful expression robbed every ounce of breath from Patricia's body. As the two tiny words sank into her consciousness, she felt joy surge through her veins. In the most ridiculously, fantastically romantic way possible, Peter was telling her he loved her! Could she offer him less?

Her decision made in an instant, Patricia launched her trembling body against his. "Oh, Peter!" Even as she cried his name she fused her mouth to his. After a startled hesitation, Peter crushed her to the hardening strength of his body.

Their lips locked in an open-mouthed kiss, they moved as one to the bed. Beside the wide bed their mouths reluctantly parted while he shrugged out of his robe and she slipped the nightgown over her head. For one brief moment they stared at one another, each delighting in and savoring the unique and individual beauty of the other. Then, moving in unison, they fell to the bed, fevered hands searching out all the previously discovered arousing areas. It had been three weeks and their hunger was mutual. Guiding him with caressing hands, Patricia brought Peter to the door of her need, then held him still until he stared into her eyes, dove-gray and softened with love for him.

"Love me, Peter," she whispered invitingly. "Make me your own."

The full meaning of her request widened his eyes, then they flared with exhilaration. "I love you, my lady ice," he vowed hoarsely. "I'll always love you."

A soft, melting smile curving her lips, Patricia drew his quivering body into the heat of hers, and his mouth to her own.

And I love you," she murmured against his lips. "Now, own me, love," she breathed, arching to him in total surrender. "And let me own you."

* * * * *